Xiaolu Guo was born in a fishing village in south China. She studied film at the Beijing Film Academy and published six books in China before moving to London in 2002. The English translation of *Village of Stone* was shortlisted for the *Independent* Foreign Fiction Prize and nominated for the IMPAC Dublin Literary Award. Her first novel written in English, *A Concise Chinese-English Dictionary for Lovers* was shortlisted for the Orange Broadband Prize for Fiction. Her most recent novel, *20 Fragments of a Ravenous Youth*, was longlisted for the Man Asian Literary Prize and her new book, *Lovers in the Age of Indifference* will be published by Chatto & Windus in 2010. Xiaolu's film career continues to flourish: her latest feature, *She, A Chinese*, was released in 2009.

Also by Xiaolu Guo

Village of Stone
A Concise Chinese-English Dictionary for Lovers
20 Fragments of a Ravenous Youth
Lovers in the Age of Indifference

UFO
in Her Eyes

XIAOLU GUO

郭小橹

VINTAGE BOOKS
London

Published by Vintage 2010

2 4 6 8 10 9 7 5 3

Copyright © Xiaolu Guo 2009

First published in Great Britain in 2009 by
Chatto & Windus
Random House, 20 Vauxhall Bridge Road,
London SW1V 2SA

www.rbooks.co.uk

Addresses for companies within The Random House Group Limited
can be found at: www.randomhouse.co.uk/offices.htm

The Random House Group Limited Reg. No. 954009

A CIP catalogue record for this book
is available from the British Library

ISBN 9780099526674

Book Design and illustration © Michael Salu

The Random House Group Limited supports The Forest Stewardship
Council® (FSC®), the leading international forest-certification organisation.
Our books carrying the FSC label are printed on FSC®-certified paper.
FSC is the only forest-certification scheme supported by the leading
environmental organisations, including Greenpeace. Our
paper procurement policy can be found at
www.randomhouse.co.uk/environment

Printed and bound in Great Britain by Clays Ltd, St Ives plc

In the beginning there was as yet no moral or social order. Men knew their mothers only, not their fathers. When hungry, they searched for food; when satisfied, they threw away the remnants. They devoured their food hide and hair, drank the blood, and clad themselves in skins and rushes. Then came Fu Xi and looked upward and contemplated the images in the heavens, and looked downward and contemplated the occurrences on earth. He united man and wife, regulated the five stages of change, and laid down the laws of humanity. He devised the eight trigrams, in order to gain mastery over the world.

Ban Gu, *White Tiger Tales*
(班固　白虎通义)

Totalitarian society, especially in its more extreme version, tends to abolish the boundary between the public and the private; power, as it grows ever more opaque, requires the lives of citizens to be entirely transparent.

Milan Kundera, *Something Behind*

Acknowledgements

I would like to thank Georges Goldenstern who, in the winter of 2007, provided me with a space to think and write, and Emmanuelle Taylor, who was so warm and helpful. To Rebecca Carter, Raymond Delambre, Clara Farmer, Claire Paterson, Michael Salu, Alison Samuel, Juliet Brooke, Pamela Casey and Philippe Ciompi – thank you for all your invaluable support.

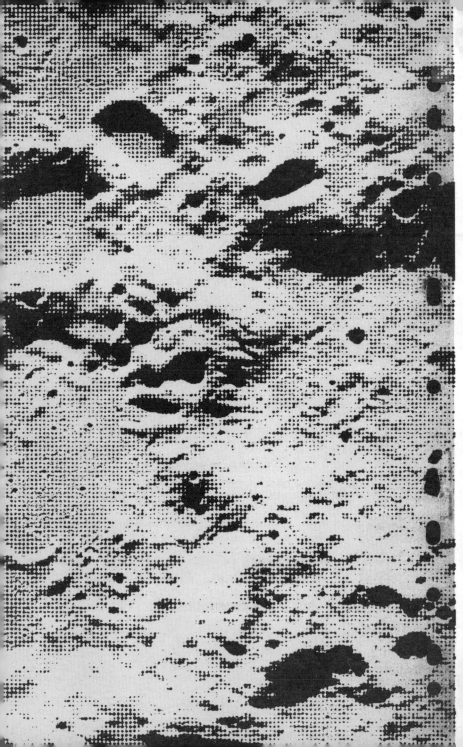

FILE
One

National Security
and Intelligence Agency
Hunan Bureau
- - - - - - - - - - -

The 09-11-2012 UFO Case

CASE START DATE:
September 2012

CASE END DATE:
Still in progress

OPERATIVES IN CHARGE:
Beijing Agent 1919 & Hunan Agent 1989

1 0 DEC 2012

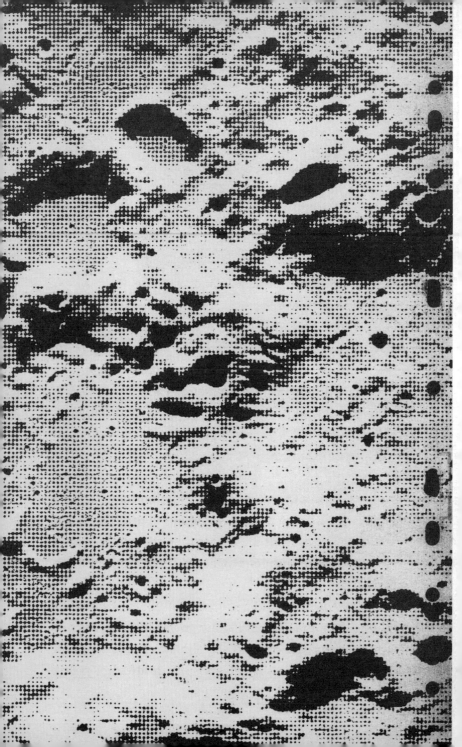

TRANSCRIPT OF INTERVIEW 001
SUBJECT: Chang Lee
       Chief of Silver Hill
INTERVIEW DATE: 14 September 2012
AGE: 52
SEX: Female
EDUCATION: Hunan Army College, Agricultural
Science Department
POLITICAL STATUS: Communist
FAMILY STATUS: Married, ███████████████

ADDRESS: Pine Soil East, Silver Hill, House 059
AGENTS PRESENT: Beijing Agent 1919; Hunan Agent 1989

BJ 1919: Right. Let's get started. Sit down please. First, can you confirm your name and status?

Have you turned your machine on? Good. I am happy for you to record everything I say. I have nothing to hide. My heart is transparent for our Communist Party.

As your higher administration knows, I am Chang Lee, Chief of Silver Hill Village. I am confident to say that, in the twenty years that I have held this position ...

BJ 1919: Thank you Chang Lee. Just respond to our questions. We'll ask you what we need to know. And please be clear. Beijing has sent me to find out what the hell has been going on here, and I don't want to hang around in this dusty, fly-ridden dump any longer than I have to.

HN 1989: Okay, okay Chief Chang, don't worry. He's cross because he had to spend three days and three nights in a bumpy army truck to get here from Beijing, and he doesn't understand our local dialect very well. I'm from the Hunan Police Department in our provincial capital Changsha. Let's start with the easy bit. Until your recent report, the Changsha Party Bureau hadn't heard from your village for a long time. Why don't you tell us a bit about Silver Hill?

Of course, of course. I always wish to do my duty.

Well, as I wanted to say before, our village is not unheard of in China. Our Great Leader Chairman Mao was born only fifteen kilometres away. I am sure the Security Agency remembers that as well as we do here.

BJ 1919: Give me a map of the village.

Please forgive us, we do not have an official map. But I can draw you one on this notepad if you will permit a humble sketch.

Comrades, as you can see, Silver Hill is a simple village, with tea and rice fields, the harvests of which are our principal source of agricultural income. There are also some non-communal, private fish farms, and a few of our peasants make hot chilli paste for additional income. The village centre is rather small, just one narrow street. But it provides everything you need in life: you can buy or sell vegetables, purchase oil, coal or light bulbs, buy your water quota, post your letters (if you are one of the villagers who can read or write, that is). We have a primary school running a non-daily class for our children.

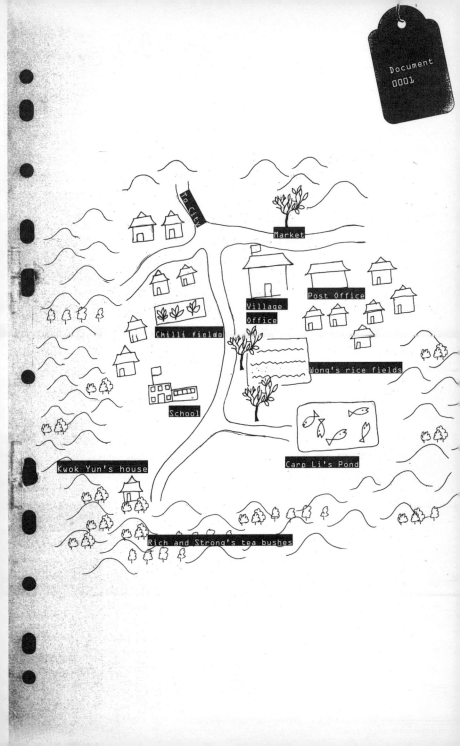

BJ 1919: Number of inhabitants?

Inhabitants? Four hundred peasants. One hundred workers. Our men and women have adhered to the One Child Policy, so our village hasn't grown because we lack young people.

The reason this place is called Silver Hill can be traced back to the Song Dynasty, no, sorry, the Yung Dynasty – 700 years ago. Or is it the Tang Dynasty, 1200 years ago? Anyway, the Imperial Chronicle, the earliest official record of this region, says that a gang named Horse Hoof ruled over the countryside, causing all the peasants to flee. According to this record, the area was a wasteland, with no vegetation or trees, only grey sand on bare hills. When the bright sun or the pale moon shone over them, the sandy hills looked silver white. And that's where the name Silver Hill came from. But I have to say that this 'silver' has not brought any wealth to our village so far.

BJ 1919: Okay, we didn't come here to listen to a history lesson. What's the situation now?

Well, I don't see how we can talk about the present day without knowing the past. But, let me try … As I told you, the most famous Chinese man in recent history – Chairman Mao – was born only fifteen kilometres away and he did wonderful things for our region. In the sixties, the Communist Party gave us a lot of attention. Our village received eight tractors and ten manure spreaders. But these machines are now past it. They have been doing their duty for decades, driving back and forth like a comb going through the same head of hair thousands of times, until the teeth of the comb begin to break and the hair starts to fall out.

BJ 1919: Are you saying you haven't received enough help from the government?

No, no, of course not. I am simply saying that, recently, our village seems to have been forgotten. When the great Mao's prestige weakened, the government support stopped. Now everything is stuck as it was in the sixties. Except it's falling apart. Once we were revolutionary and progressive, now we are slow and backward. The tractors have rusted, the soil has turned sour, and the peasants have started to moan. Imagine my position as Chief of such a place!

What can I tell you about the villagers? We are from the hilly south-west of China, you see. Of the six hundred million Chinese peasants, we must be among the poorest. It is said in our nation that one must learn how to 'eat bitterness'. Well, that's about all we eat in this village. The last time we shed tears was thirty-six years ago, when Chairman Mao died. On that day, every villager wept, everyone from five to ninety-five. But since then, we can't be bothered to cry. Cry for what? Three hundred people from this village died of starvation during the Great Leap Forward, we saw their corpses floating in the lake. Our tears dried in our throats. We had to eat grass and roots to survive. And now the kids can afford to drink their useless coca cola.

Yes. Taking each day at a time, getting up at dawn to work in the brown fields and returning home under the moon-lit sky: that is life in Silver Hill. What really surprises us is to find ourselves still alive when we wake up in the morning.

BJ 1919: Okay, I'm hungry. I saw a noodle stall out there. Let's stop the tape.

TRANSCRIPT OF INTERVIEW 002
SUBJECT: Zhao Ning
          Secretary to Chief Chang
INTERVIEW DATE: 14 September 2012
AGE: 45
SEX: Male
EDUCATION: Wen Hua Township High School
POLITICAL STATUS: Communist
FAMILY STATUS: Married; no children
ADDRESS: Pine Soil East, Silver Hill, House 036
AGENTS PRESENT: Beijing Agent 1919; Hunan Agent 1989

HN 1989: Sorry to keep you waiting Secretary Zhao. My colleague needed to take a break. Is there anything particular you think we should know about Silver Hill before we start our investigation?

First may I say, it is an honour to have you here. And I am glad you can see for yourselves the excellence of Chief Chang. I have been working as her secretary for fifteen years and so I know all about this village. She is a mighty woman, who guides us all with her very great education. Never does she let her own personal interests interfere with her civic duty.

For your information, I want to add three points about Silver Hill. I promise you, everything I say is true:

Firstly, in the sixties, we had one 'Man Eats Man' incident. I see shock in your faces, Comrades. But you are young so perhaps I should explain it to you. In the late fifties, the government encouraged the whole population of China to focus on industry in the Great Leap Forward – 'More, Better, Faster, Cheaper' was one of the slogans. But then, all over the nation, crops failed due to flooding followed by drought. In this region we suffered a plague of locusts. As a result, mass starvation arose. There was nothing left to eat. People had to eat grass. In this province, two thirds of the population died. If you study our village archives from that time, you will find a record of how Jin Yichuan cooked and ate his dead brother's leg in order to escape his own death. Yes. Don't stare at me like that, Comrades, these things can happen in such times.

This place is still nearly as poor as then, but at least we don't have to eat each other any more.

Secondly, in 1961, our butcher was named 'Parasite Eradication Hero' for ridding our fields of of sparrows.

Thirdly, I must tell you about our Hundred Arm trees. They are the pride of our village. When you pass, please admire their strong branches, which plunge down into the ground and then rise out of the soil again some distance away. These trees have survived wars, revolutions, droughts. There is one by the Chow Mein King's noodle stall in the market, and two by Wong's rice fields. The one by the noodle stall is about 250 years old. Even from a distance you can see its creeping branches. It looks like a giant with hundreds of arms. Sorry to take so much of your time talking about three trees, but you know, in Silver Hill we have few things more precious.

BJ 1919: Why? Do they produce a valuable fruit?

No, these trees don't grow fruit. But isn't the past a fruit to enjoy? Our great-grandfathers grew up under these trees, and I spent my childhood playing under their green shade.

As Chief Chang says, 'We can't talk about the present without knowing the past.'

BJ 1919: Dog Sun, you've got a strange sense of value. No wonder this is a fucking backwater. Plus you're all breeding like rabbits. Despite what Chief Chang says, it doesn't look as if there's much obedience to the One Child Policy round here. Perhaps I should send over some inspectors ...

Comrade, I cannot comment on that. Personally speaking, one child would be enough for me. My wife and I have done everything we can to conceive a child – eaten thousands of lotus seeds, drunk many bottles of snake liquor, prayed to Guan Shi Yin, the Goddess Ma Zu – and still we have had no luck. No fruit, no value. That's your view, isn't it? Well, at least my wife and I have had each other during these tough times. I don't blame her…

BJ 1919: Okay, okay, I didn't come here to listen to your sob story. Let's call it a day.

TRANSCRIPT OF INTERVIEW 003
SUBJECT: Kwok Yun
INTERVIEW DATE: 15 September 2012
AGE: 37
SEX: Female
EDUCATION: Illiterate
POLITICAL STATUS: Peasant
FAMILY STATUS: Unmarried; lives with grandfather
ADDRESS: Cat Knot Pathway, Silver Hill, House 099
AGENTS PRESENT: Beijing Agent 1919; Hunan Agent 1989

BJ 1919: Dog Sun, are you sure we've got the right person here? If I didn't have this woman's ID card in front of me, I'd think she was a bloke!

HN 1989: I'm sure. This is definitely the house we were directed to. It's the only one so far out of the village.

BJ 1919: Too right, it's far. I thought the truck was going to be shaken to bits driving down that track.

Sit down Kwok Yun, you can't answer questions properly if you're shuffling from foot to foot. Now concentrate. Firstly, do you recognise this statement by Chief Chang?

Can you do me a favour and speak more slowly. Your Beijing language is difficult for me to understand.

HN 1989: Here, let me read it to her in dialect.

> At around midday on Tuesday, 11 September 2012, Silver Hill peasant Kwok Yun saw in the sky above Wong's rice fields a flying metal plate that we can only assume to be a UFO …

So, do you recognise that?

Yes, I do. But I don't understand why you can't just ask Chief Chang about it. I've told her everything already.

BJ 1919: Silence. Remember you're talking to the police. Regardless of what Chief Chang has said, we need a first-hand account from you. Let's start with your family background. You live with your grandfather?

Yes, my name is Yun and I live with my grandfather Old Kwok. He runs a 'five metals' stall on the market, selling all the hammers, nails and tools that our villagers need. I help him with the stall and with the house.

BJ 1919: Where are your parents?

Dead.

BJ 1919: How and when?

Hmm … It was soon after I was born. I was told they died

14

under a truck. It was carrying coal and was coming through our hills from some northern province. The road was wet and the truck skidded and fell down the hillside. The driver was killed too ... I heard that everybody came and took the coal home. They cooked all their meals with it for days to come.

BJ 1919: And what happened on the day you saw the UFO?

What was it you called that flying metal plate again? A UFO? That's what Chief Chang called it too. I'd never heard that word before.

I don't remember much from that day. It was the Twentieth Day of the Seventh Moon, the calendar said it was the luckiest day in the whole month. So I thought it might bring me good fortune. But ...

BJ 1919: Okay, okay, enough of that claptrap. I had a lifetime's supply of it from my mother, even though the Cultural Revolution banned it. What I want to know is did you feel anything unusual that morning, any physical pain, a headache?

Hmm ... I don't know if I should mention these trivial women's things in front of the People's Police ...

BJ 1919: Nothing is too trivial for the police. You must give us all the details.

Well ... that morning, my bleeding started. A real curse for women. Did that have anything to do with the UFO? I don't know. What I do know is that my stomach ached like hell and my back hurt. You want the details? I'll tell you. When I bleed, I feel like one of the earthworms grandfather used to chop in half with his spade when he had his chive patch: an earthworm who has lost its tail, bleeding in the dark soil without anyone caring for its pain. You know how those dark-brown worms have two blood vessels running through their bodies, one that takes the blood to the tail, the other that pumps it back to the head? Well, that's exactly what was going on inside my body that day – blood pumping through me like water out of a burst tap. I could feel the speed of the flowing blood and it was like torture.

My face was yellow and I was sure that, in the hot sun, people could smell my blood. The old women in the village tell me that period pain isn't so bad after a woman gets married, and after she gives birth it goes away completely. Why do they tell me this when I haven't got a husband? Those mean bitches. All the women in this cursed village are bitches. That's why, since Carp Li's daughter left, I've never had another friend. A rich man from the south took her away to marry her. I hope she's living in a big city house with a washing machine and a fridge and all those white plastic things that I see on Chief Chang's television. She deserves it. She used to bring me ice sticks to eat when I was standing all day at grandfather's market stall under the hot, poisonous sun. The others just ignored me. The people here are merciless.

•

BJ 1919: You must stop these negative views about other people. It does no good to you and wastes time. You should listen to the old women and get married.

Who would I marry? All the young men have left this village. They are more wedded to that fertiliser of theirs than they are to women. The price of fertiliser is much higher than the price of rice so they think there's money to be made selling it in the big cities. Any big city is better than Silver Hill. And even if there were any bachelors left, who would want me? I am ugly, I know that, at least that's what people tell me. And you can see I am not young any more. Why do I need a man anyway? I've survived by myself so far, I can't see why a man should be necessary. You mean children? There are already too many brats in this village. They are like the unharvested potatoes rotting away in the fields. The sun here makes everything decay. It beats down on sticky skin, sweaty legs, burning hair, muddy arms, dead leaves, broken roots, old seeds, and slowly they all rot. I hate this place.

HN 1989: Stop the tape. Can't you see the woman's shaking? Don't let's push her any more now.

BJ 1919: Dog Sun, you're so soft. How did you ever make it into the police?

TRANSCRIPT OF INTERVIEW 004
SUBJECT: Kwok Yun
INTERVIEW DATE: 15 September 2012
AGE: 37
SEX: Female
EDUCATION: Illiterate
POLITICAL STATUS: Peasant
FAMILY STATUS: Unmarried; lives with grandfather
ADDRESS: Cat Knot Pathway, Silver Hill, House 099
AGENTS PRESENT: Beijing Agent 1919; Hunan Agent 1989

HN 1989: Are you feeling better, Old Sister? Two hours ago we had to break off our interview because you were feeling unwell. Please can you now start again, telling us every detail of what you saw on that day.

It was the Twentieth Day of the Seventh Moon, according to the calendar we use. In the morning I went to the village to get some sugar and rice. As you can see, our house is not in the village, it stands alone. To get to the village, I have to cycle over the hill and along Cat Knot Pathway. It takes me a while.

So I went out with my bicycle. The rest, you already know. I passed Wong's rice fields, then I saw that flying metal plate – the UFO, as you call it.

HN 1989: We need details, Old Sister. What you did before you left the house, the route you took to Wong's rice fields, that kind of thing.

Before I left the house I put on my red T-shirt, the one with the funny foreign writing on the front. I like it because it's the only thing I've ever bought in a department store. I got it four years ago when I went to town with my grandfather to celebrate the Olympics. That was a great moment for China, wasn't it? Chief Chang bought ten TVs for the village so we could all witness it. I went to her office to see what the blond foreigners looked like. And of course I watched the gymnastics and the diving – the Chinese team is always the best.

BJ 1919: Okay, forget about the Olympics and what you were wearing. What did you do next?

Then I must have pumped up the tyres on my old Flying Pigeon bicycle. I have to pump them up each time I use it.

Riding my old Flying Pigeon, I passed the two little hills where farmer Rich and Strong grows his tea, then I arrived at Wong's rice fields, which were half-harvested. The smell of rice mixed with the fragrance of tea plants made me dizzy. I got off my bicycle and sat on a stone to drink some water from my bottle. I was so thirsty I felt as if I could drink up all the water beneath the soil. The scorching sun was sucking out my energy, my head was empty. Maybe you'll think it's stupid, but sometimes I picture myself as a small tea bush, or a grain of rice, or a leaf on one of the Hundred Arm trees. That's what I felt like then.

HN 1989: Interesting. But can you tell us precisely what happened just before you saw the UFO?

So … I was sitting on that stone with the sweat pouring down my face, feeling completely weak, when suddenly I sensed a weird power all around me and heard a strange sound coming from the sky. The sound grew louder and louder, and I felt that a strong force was going to pull me into the air, the way a river whirlpool pulls in a leaf. I'd never heard anything like that noise. I looked at the sky, but I was blinded by sunlight. Then I got scared and I ran over to the shade of the Hundred Arm tree.

While I was standing there, trying to figure out what the noise might be, I could feel my bowels cramping like a dying fish, I was bleeding so much. Then, all of a sudden, a large silver plate appeared in the sky and flew towards the Hundred Arm tree. At first I thought it must be a daydream. But then I realised that the noise was coming from the enormous metal plate. I stared at it, terrified. It was as if I was a tiny insect, exposed on the soil, about to be eaten by a big bird. I kept gazing at that white monster, and suddenly the world in front of me went hazy and I collapsed.

HN 1989: Did you see the foreigner before or after you collapsed?

Afterwards. As I told Chief Chang, I don't know how long I slept for. I woke up among the roots of the Hundred Arm tree, my body covered in a layer of leaves. A red beetle was sitting on my left arm, ants were travelling in my hair. I sat up empty-minded and looked at the sky, but there was nothing there, only a few clouds floating silently by, and the same painful sun. I was about to leave when I heard an odd

See Interviews 005-011. Apart from Mad Woman Lin Shi, Kwok Yun is the only person who heard a loud noise between 11:00 and 13:00

noise in the grass, like someone pulling themselves along the ground and breathing heavily. Anxiously, I looked over and saw a body lying a few metres away among the half-harvested rice plants.

What I saw was a foreigner, a real foreigner with deep eye holes, sun-burnt skin and grass-coloured hair. He looked in terrible pain, but he seemed harmless. He said something and tried to sit up. I saw that one of his legs had a wound and it was bleeding. Beneath his leather sandal, the foot was swollen. I thought: 'Today is supposed to be the luckiest day in the month, but actually everyone is bleeding. It's a day of blood!'

The foreigner stared at me like a huge rabbit. He mumbled some words, and then his eyes moved towards my red T-shirt. Maybe he was reading the Western characters on my front, but I blushed like a beetroot I can tell you. No one has ever stared at my chest like that! Then suddenly the big noisy flying machine jumped back into my mind: 'Maybe there are other foreigners,' I thought to myself. 'But why here?' I looked around, fearing an army of yellow-haired, blue-eyed foreigners looking at my breasts. But no, there was only this one lying in old Wong's field.

HN 1989: Why did you take him to your home?

Officer, as you well know, in China there are only foreigners in big cities like Beijing or Shanghai, certainly not here, in lousy Silver Hill! So I thought: a Chinese peasant cannot let a foreigner die, or let him remain injured. It would be a political mistake. I was thinking: 'If I don't save him, I will be accused of harming the friendship between China and some powerful foreign country.' Maybe he was from the ex-Soviet Union! How could I know? Plus, I believe you should never be cold-hearted. So I decided to help him, however I could. But even using all my strength, I only managed to pull him a little way out of the rice field. He was lying on the dusty road with his hurt foot, like a dead plant.

HN 1989: You told Chief Chang you were helped by some children. Did the kids find you, or did you go and fetch them?

They found me. They were running through the fields like a swarm of flies, all dirty and sweaty with runny noses. They were throwing stones at each other as they ran, but as soon as they saw the man lying in the dust, they stopped.

A girl was the first to notice. 'Oh! He is a foreigner!' she screamed. Then another kid asked whether he was dying. Someone else asked if he could understand what we were saying. One boy said: 'The foreigner can definitely understand our language. Foreigners are much cleverer than us. Maybe he's a scientist.' Then another boy argued that the foreigner must be a football player since he was two metres tall. (If you really want to know the facts, I think he measured about 190 centimetres.)

HN 1989: Who, in your opinion, was the foreigner?

How do I know?

My grandfather told me that a foreign priest once visited the province, so I thought he might be some priest. Anyway I had to find a way to cure his foot. So I called the kids to help me, and in the end we managed to get him to my house.

And that afternoon, in the kitchen, after I had given him some Yunan powder and bandaged his leg with my grandfather's old shirt, the foreigner managed to smile and stand up. He spoke a string of odd words. I think he was trying to say thank you. But I wanted to fetch some herbal medicine for him before it got too late. That's what I explained to him. I poured him some tea, then I ran out. Twenty minutes later, when I came back, he had disappeared.

I looked at the tea on the table. It was still warm. My foreigner had gone. After sitting on my bench for a while, I realised that I had to report the whole matter to Chief Chang without delay, so I immediately left the house again. That was at about three in the afternoon.

HN 1989: Okay, I think we can stop there. We've got everything we need.

BJ 1919: Dog Sun, you may think you've got everything you need. I hardly understood a word. Your fucking dialect is incomprehensible.

HN 1989: I think we should go and talk to other villagers to find out if anyone else heard this noise.

24

From: Beijing Agent 1919

Sent: 16 September 2012 17:16

To: Senior Officer ▉▉▉

Subject: The 09-11-2012 UFO Case

Dear Senior Officer ▉▉▉

I have now been in Silver Hill Village for three days and have conducted a number of interviews with the peasants, assisted by the local police. However, since the villagers have virtually no understanding of our Beijing language and are only able to talk in dialect, I have concluded that it would be better for Hunan Agent 1989 to interview the villagers alone. I know these local policemen aren't the brightest of people, but if I brief him properly, he can ask the questions in dialect and then translate the interviews for me. In the meantime, I will make an extensive examination of the area in which the UFO was sighted.

I hereby salute you,

Beijing Agent 1919

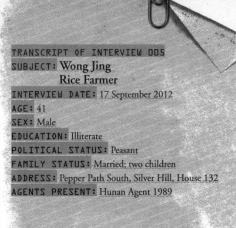

TRANSCRIPT OF INTERVIEW 005
SUBJECT: Wong Jing
          Rice Farmer
INTERVIEW DATE: 17 September 2012
AGE: 41
SEX: Male
EDUCATION: Illiterate
POLITICAL STATUS: Peasant
FAMILY STATUS: Married; two children
ADDRESS: Pepper Path South, Silver Hill, House 132
AGENTS PRESENT: Hunan Agent 1989

HN 1989: Hello, Comrade, please tell me your status.

What?

HN 1989: Your status!

What is a 'status'?

HN 1989: Okay, tell me your name, age, job, family members, and whether you, too, witnessed the UFO.

I am Wong Jing. I am forty-one. I own the rice field where this girl Yun says some UFO thing landed. But I have nothing to report to you, Comrade. I was the last person to know about it. Is it true? What is a UFO anyway?

At this time of year, I am so busy with my rice, I don't have time for anything else. I have two fields, and I have to work day and night to finish storing the grain before the autumn rots my crops. On that afternoon, me and my wife were in the yard removing the husks from the milled rice. We had our kids with us. They had skipped school to help, even though Headmaster Yee wasn't pleased about it. We heard nothing and saw nothing, either in the sky or wherever. So I know nothing. All I can say is that it was perhaps the hottest day I have ever suffered in my dog's life. My kid told me the radio said it was forty-two degrees. Could that be somehow linked to the UFO? Perhaps a UFO is like a hotwater boiler that heats the sky … Do you remember the tale of Hou Yi who shot the 'Nine Suns'? No? Did your grandfather never tell you that? Maybe that's because you are from the modern city, unlike us. We only know old stories like that. I'll tell you. Long long ago there was not one sun, but ten Sun-birds. They were the sons of the Emperor of the Eastern Heaven. Each morning, one of these Sun-birds had to rise and give light to the world. One day, the Sun-birds wanted a change and decided all to rise at once. The heat on earth became so unbearable that the humans started to die and the plants to burn. So the Emperor of the Eastern Heaven ordered Hou Yi, the Immortal Archer, to teach a lesson to his ten naughty sons. Hou Yi was a great archer. He lifted his mighty bow and shot the suns down one by one. He left only one sun in the sky so the world got back to normal. But the Emperor was so angry with Hou Yi for killing his sons that he punished him, making him live on the earth as a mere mortal. Bitch Bastard! Did that old Emperor not understand who saved the earth!

What else can I tell you? This year is supposed to be the Year of the Dragon, a powerful, good year, but there has not been enough water for our rice fields, so the harvest is bad.

Just look around here, you can tell it's going to become a desert. You, the police, should come back in five years' time and check whether this village still exists. Heaven should rehabilitate Hou Yi, the Immortal Archer, so he can return again to save us.

What else? You want me to talk about UFOs? I've never seen one. And I guess if I had seen one, I wouldn't want to talk about it. What's all the fuss about? Is a UFO useful for us? I have to go and polish my rice now. My wife is alone in the yard and she'll curse me for eternity if I don't move my arse.

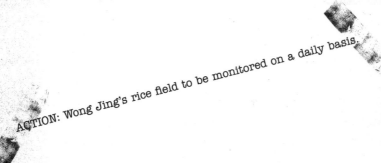

ACTION: Wong Jing's rice field to be monitored on a daily basis.

TRANSCRIPT OF INTERVIEW 006
SUBJECT: **Fu Qiang (Rich and Strong)**
Tea Farmer
INTERVIEW DATE: 17 September 2012
AGE: 62
SEX: Male
EDUCATION: Illiterate
POLITICAL STATUS: Peasant
FAMILY STATUS: Married; one son
ADDRESS: Sparrow Ditch, Silver Hill, House 78
AGENTS PRESENT: Hunan Agent 1989

HN 1989: Tell me your status.

My status? My name is Fu Qiang, but in the village they call me 'Rich and Strong', although I'm poorer than any bastard rat in the tea fields. I'm a peasant tea farmer. But I've got the potential to be a good citizen, I know I have. Look at my son. He's an accountant in Shanghai now. Bitch Bastard! We've got open minds in this family, Officer, unlike the other idiot peasants in this village who live only for their fields.

HN 1989: Chief Chang tells us that you saw Kwok Yun just before she encountered the UFO, is that right?

Yes, I saw Old Kwok's granddaughter Yun that day – the Twentieth Day of the Seventh Moon. But I didn't see any flying metal plate, and I didn't hear any special noise either. I only saw Yun. It was around noon, probably just before she got to Wong's fields.

She was riding her lousy old bicycle, you know that white 'Flying Pigeon' bicycle her grandfather bought for her ages ago. She and her bicycle are as one, they go everywhere together. But it's falling apart, that Flying Pigeon, and she's always complaining about the punctures. Half the time she's at the market trying to get it fixed by the bike mender. She must spend more time with that bike mender than she does looking after her grandfather. If you ask me, that Bitch Bastard migrant should learn to speak our dialect or fuck off back to where he came from. How can you work somewhere when you can't talk to anyone?

HN 1989: Okay, okay, we don't care about the bicycle and the bike mender. Just tell me what you saw that day.

Hmm ... actually, now I come to think about it, I wonder if it was on that day that I saw her. Perhaps it was the day before, which was National Wiping Out Illiteracy Day. I went to Chief Chang's office to listen to her weekly commentary on the news. She reads her newspapers and then explains to us what is going on in the world. That day, she told us that ███████ are still illiterate. That makes me one of ██████████. Anyway that's when I saw Yun on her bicycle – when I was on my way to Chief Chang's. But maybe I saw her the day after too. I often see her on that lonely stretch of road.

HN 1989: Perhaps if we call in your wife from the fields, she might be able to help us clear up which day it was?

My wife? Are you joking? She can't clear up the yard. Bitch Bastard! No point talking to her. Listen, if you want to know anything in this village, you've got to talk to the men. Chief Chang excepted of course. In her family, she wears the trousers.

HN 1989: All right, let's forget about your wife. Assuming you did see Yun on that day, did you notice anything unusual or suspicious in her behaviour?

Well, how can I put this … I wouldn't want to say anything bad about my old friend's granddaughter. It would be shameful for me, you understand? But when Yun rides down the hill on her rickety old bike, you'd think she was a man. I don't want to say she's ugly, mind you. No, it's just that she's so stocky. What's more, years of fieldwork under the burning sun have made her cheeks as dark as autumn dates. She keeps her hair short, like a good socialist peasant, and her hands and feet are so enormous they scare men away. Okay, in the sixties and seventies it was considered a virtue for a woman to look plain. In those days, people would say things like: 'She's such a modest person, she must have a beautiful heart inside.' But nowadays, Bitch Bastard, even a poor man wants a pretty woman, not a woman with big hands and elephant feet. Yun is built like a tree, solid and earthy. I don't think she can even wear women's shoes. She needs a size forty-one, everyone knows that. And she has a problem finding Extra Large clothes, so for years now she's just been wearing men's clothes. It's not surprising she hasn't got married. A manly woman is like an earthworm: both male and female in one body. Yes, a giant earthworm, that's what Yun is. I feel sorry for her and Old Kwok.

Anyway, whenever it was that I saw her, I didn't notice anything unusual. Bitch Bastard, I've got to do something to straighten out my brain. I'm thirsty. Can I have some water from your bottle?

TRANSCRIPT OF INTERVIEW 007
SUBJECT: Kwok Zidong (Old Kwok)
Stall Holder
INTERVIEW DATE: 18 September 2012
AGE: 80
SEX: Male
EDUCATION: Illiterate
POLITICAL STATUS: Peasant
FAMILY STATUS: Widower (wife died 1961); lives with granddaughter
ADDRESS: Cat Knot Pathway, Silver Hill, House 099
AGENTS PRESENT: Hunan Agent 1989

HN 1989: as I understand it, you are the grandfather of the young woman who claims to have seen a UFO, Kwok Yun. Is this correct?

What do you want? People tell me my granddaughter saw a strange plate in the sky. So what is that Bitch Bastard story all about, eh? Has everybody turned mad? I understand nothing of this modern world. I've never done a bad deed in my life, so don't waste your time trying to dig anything out of my knotted brain. Besides, I stopped thinking long ago. Thinking doesn't do anybody any good. The more you think, the more you get into trouble. During the Cultural Revolution you could even go to prison for it. No, I've given up on this Bitch Bastard world. All I can tell you is that, on the morning when my granddaughter is supposed to have seen this flying plate, I looked at the calendar on my wall (our proper peasant calendar, not your impossible city people's Western thing) and it said that it was a day for 'opening houses and going to the fields', and that 'closing doors and drinking spirits' would bring bad luck. So I didn't close our

35

door and, on my way to the market, I took the long route through the tea fields. But I have to confess that … I drank some sorghum wine. I shouldn't have done that, should I?

HN 1989: Where were you and what were you doing at noon, when the UFO appeared?

Did I not tell that to your colleague from Beijing already? The one with the square head who spends his whole time at Niu Ping's liquor stall drinking Er Guo Tou while you do all the work? Did he not understand what I said or something?

HN 1989: Respect the police! I'm the one asking the questions here.

Waste of time … Anyway, as I told your colleague, I went to the Chow Mein King's noodle stall to eat the biggest Bitch Bastard bowl of noodles I could get. I hadn't had any breakfast. My granddaughter had her monthly bleeding and she'd slept in instead of cooking breakfast. By lunch time, I was so hungry I couldn't move an inch. My sight was blurred, I was sweating like a hog. I dragged myself to the noodle stall, cursing everything in front of my eyes – the Hundred Arm tree, the rooster, the passing buffaloes, even the noodle maker. Bitch Bastard Sun!

Have you met our noodle maker? We call him the Chow Mein King, since his surname 'Wang' means 'king'. For the last two decades he has spent every day making dough and frying Chow Mein. Even on the day his wife died, he only left his stall for a few hours.

HN 1989: Tell me exactly what you said to each other.

I can't remember that. What do you think we old peasants talk about? Nothing worth writing down, I can tell you.

What's for sure, that bastard noodle-maker managed to convince me to have beef instead of pork. He always decides what his customers should eat. As soon as you arrive, he starts cooking, and there it is: beef Chow Mein. Beef is twice as expensive as pork, the filthy bastard, but then again, it is delicious. That noodle man is a true miser, he'd rather let his beef rot than lower his prices.

But at least he knows his job: the noodles arrived instantly, and at once they slipped into my old stomach. What a relief! Heaven knows why I'm always so hungry! Maybe I've eaten too much chilli in my life. Everyone knows this region of ours is famous in the big world for its chilli powder. The more chilli one eats, the hungrier and more aggressive one becomes, don't you agree? Perhaps I should eat a bit less of it. What do you think? When I was young, I thought that growing old would bring greater satisfaction. But it's always the same Bitch Bastard thing. Satisfaction is impossible for a man who's always hungry. Do you understand what I'm talking about?

Anyway, it was good food that day, and it was cooling to be in the shade of the tree. After the beef noodles, I had a little nap among its hundred arms. In my half sleep, I started to wonder … Who am I? What year is it? Where am I? And why am I ageing like this? Then I woke up. I tried to think back through my time, the time I have been living. But then I gave up. Bitch Bastard, I said to myself, nothing matters except food. Even good weather doesn't brighten my life. Since I stopped growing my chives, years ago, I don't care about the weather any more. As long as I can carry on running my little 'five metals' stall, and have rice or noodles for my next meal, my life is not a dog's life. One should not complain, an old man should be wise. 'Eat bitterness': people have been saying that for thousands of years.

HN 1989: Tell me about your relationship with your granddaughter.

If you really want to know, there's only one thing that prevents me from dying and that is worrying about Yun. I worry about her all the time. You probably don't know her much. She's already over thirty, and without a husband. Where will I find her one? In Silver Hill, there are only old buffaloes like me left, the young men all went to the cities. Cities must be great, eh? Otherwise why don't they come back? Poor girl. I can't see how I'll be able to find her a man before I go to my grave.

Yun is all I have in my life. Her grandmother died during the Great Famine. Then, when she was a baby, her mother and father died in an accident. I had to feed the little girl with my own hands.

They've all been gone so long I can't remember their faces. Maybe that's not so important, but I really miss their voices.

I would like to hear someone's voice talking to me during the long nights. I am old, I don't sleep much any more. Very often I wake up at four in the morning, and can't go back to sleep. When that happens, I just go out and walk through the hills to my market stall, with the moon caressing my shoulder. As I walk, I try to remember the things my wife and my daughter used to say, hoping that through their words I'll be able to hear their voices. But they are lost in the spider's web entangling my heart. I cannot remember anything. Were their voices like Yun's? Did they smile when they were alive? In Silver Hill, we don't smile much. Smiling is even more difficult than crying. Our faces have been frozen by hardship. You understand what I am saying? Yun doesn't smile. She doesn't talk much either. She just listens to my swearing and cooks my food. What goes on in her broad forehead, I don't know.

List of Traders in Silver Village: supplied to Hunan Agent 1989 by Chief Chang

Five Metals Stall: Kwok Zidong
Noodle Stall: Wang Ming
Butcher's Stall: Ling Zhu
Bicycle Stall: Migrant worker, name unknown
Liquor Stall: Niu Ping
Rice and Flour Stall: Jiang Linjun
Vegetable Stall: Ma Liang
Cobbler: Rao Yun
Key Maker: Li Yin
Stationery Stall: Bao Tian
Palm Reader: Cheng Dasheng

TRANSCRIPT OF INTERVIEW 008
SUBJECT: Ling Zhu
        Butcher
INTERVIEW DATE: 18 September 2012
AGE: 65
SEX: Male
EDUCATION: Illiterate
POLITICAL STATUS: Peasant
FAMILY STATUS: Married; one son; lives alone
ADDRESS: Butcher's stall, Market Street, Silver Hill
AGENTS PRESENT: Hunan Agent 1989

HN 1989: Your name and age?

Ling Zhu. You tell me how old I am! Chief Chang says I'm sixty-five this year, but who knows if that's right?. I was an orphan, and the authorities told me I was born at the end of the forties. So I let you decide my age.

HN 1989: It's not up to me to decide your age. We aren't living in the feudal era any more.

But I don't care what age I am.

HN 1989: What do you mean you don't care? China is now a democratic country. It's your responsibility to know your age.

Don't spit on my pork, you young rat! If you want, I'll say I was born in 1947, because I like the number seven.

HN 1989; Okay, okay. So where do you live?

Here. I live and sleep here in this shed, in the middle of the market. It's convenient since I have to be here every day selling my pork. I slaughter my pigs in the yard. If you're going to ask me about that UFO, I can tell you now, I know nothing about it. If it came and hovered over my place, I didn't see it. I must have been killing a pig, or sleeping. Cow's Cunt! Those are the only things I care about.

HN 1989: So people are right when they say you're a bit of a moody type ...

Who said that? The bastards! This place stinks. Everyone wants to eat good meat, nobody wants to pay for it, and then they badmouth you behind your back. Bastards.

HN 1989: Okay, calm down. This isn't important. Tell me, is it right that you were once famous for killing parasites, back in the sixties?

You want to know my sparrow story? That's a surprise. Here in Silver Hill no one can stand it any more. But if you really want to hear it, I'm happy to tell it, and you'll see that I'm not really as bad-tempered as those bastards say.

It was during the Great Leap Forward, when Chairman Mao was helping China catch up with Western Industry. Crops were failing because sparrows were eating all the seeds, so Chairman Mao decided that we peasants should go around banging pots and pans to scare them away from the fields. Now, I was young and speedy, Cow's Cunt, and

42

I didn't have the patience to bang pots. What's more, I was sharp-eyed, and a dab hand with a gun. I thought it would be more clever to shoot those bastard parasite birds. So I got a rifle from the local militia, and shot down ninety-six sparrows in one day, and eighty-three the next, and took the corpses to the local Party office. Because of my work, I was granted the 'Parasite Eradication Hero' medal by the government.

HN 1989: There are those that think such medals shouldn't have been awarded. After all, following the Great Sparrow Campaign, locusts swarmed the whole country because there were no sparrows to eat them, and that's how the Great Famine started. According to China's Disaster Centre, two million people died of starvation in 1962, right after the Great Sparrow Campaign. You must know that.

Who are the bastards who dare say the famine was my fault? I'll swear on Chairman Mao's dead soul that your life will end here if you say that kind of thing again, even though you wear that police uniform! I'll tell you one thing: rats eat as many locusts as stupid sparrows. And what about chickens? Cow's Cunt! Chickens are the biggest locust eaters there are. No one can deny I was the greatest parasite killer this province has ever seen, and everyone knows about my contribution to the Great Leap Forward! At that time, you were perhaps not even born, young man. Can I ask your age?

You will probably be happy to know that I'm a nobody now, just the bad-tempered village butcher, as they say. I don't have sharp eyes any more. And I have no patience for anything either. I have a wife and a son but they live with my wife's family in the neighbouring village. They don't like Silver Hill. No one likes this place. And I can't be bothered to visit them. She's given me a son, that's good enough.

What else can I say? I've been selling pork in this market for forty-five years. I don't eat fruit and vegetables. Why should I? My pigs are under my nose every day. I slaughter one pig every two weeks, more during Spring Festival. A fat pig weighs 120 kilos, a small one 70 kilos. If each family in Silver Hill eats one kilo of pork every day, that makes exactly one big pig every two weeks. Do you follow me? We in Silver Hill are quick at counting. Anyway, my life is not bad – each sow has eight to twelve piglets, so Silver Hill can count on my pork for the next twenty years. What else do you need to know?

It's hard to remember. It was very hot. Chief Chang's husband passed by to get some belly of pork … I had a snooze … Then I had a conversation with Old Kwok, who came to get pigs' feet. I don't know what was up with him. Afterwards he wandered over to the Hundred Arm tree looking upset. As though he'd seen a ghost.

HN 1989: Okay. We can stop here for today.

TRANSCRIPT OF INTERVIEW 009
SUBJECT: Yee Ming
Headmaster of Primary School
INTERVIEW DATE: 19 September 2012
AGE: 49
SEX: Male
EDUCATION: Changsha Normal College, Maths Department
POLITICAL STATUS: Communist
FAMILY STATUS: Unmarried
ADDRESS: Primary School, Silver Hill
AGENTS PRESENT: Hunan Agent 1989

HN 1989: Excuse me, Headmaster, but are you busy?

As you can see, the school is closed today so I can spare you a little time. How can I help you?

HN 1989: We are interested to know if, around noon on 11 September, you heard any unusually loud noise.

If, as I imagine is the case, you are referring to noise made by a possible UFO, then I can assure you that I didn't. The only loud noise I heard at noon was the shouting of children as they left the school for the day. Unfortunately, in this poor village, we cannot afford to run our school on a full-time basis.

HN 1989: Can you describe the school curriculum. Do you ever discuss space travel?

Certainly not. Such things are only taught in High School.

The discussion of black holes, supernovas and other elements of the planetary system can be detrimental to the young mind, and overly political. No, at Silver Hill Primary School, I stick largely to mathematics. It is well known that the inhabitants of this village are exceptionally good with numbers, so I make a special effort to support our pupils in that field, so they can hope to enter either the Accountancy College or Technical College of our province capital, thus contributing to science and technology with their talents. I put particular emphasis on Euclid's *Elements* and his five common laws. I think they should learn those laws as early as possible. If you look at the blackboard, you will see that I have written them up there:

1. *Things that equal the same thing also equal one another.*
2. *If equals are added to equals, then the sums are equal.*
3. *If equals are subtracted from equals, the remainders are equal.*
4. *Things that coincide with one another equal one another.*
5. *The whole is greater than the part.*

And I teach younger kids about Perfect Numbers. For example, that the first perfect number is 6 because of its positive divisors 1 + 2 + 3, and that the second perfect number is 28 (because 28 = 1 + 2 + 4 + 7 + 14) and that the next perfect numbers are 496, 8128, etc. Of course I also teach them about Prime Numbers. I really like Prime Numbers because they are the most independent: they can divide only by one and by themselves, like 2, 3, 5, 7, 11, 13, 17, 19, 23, 29, etc.

HN 1989: Don't you think that what you teach your pupils is a little beyond their capacities?

I don't think so. Don't underestimate Silver Hill's arithmetical capacities. You may call it an obsession, but as an educationalist, I have an obligation to develop innate talent, and take it to higher levels. It must not be allowed to go to waste, even if it ends up being used only to calculate the weight of pork or count grains of rice. I am confident that by pushing the boundaries, Silver Hill pupils will become truly talented and be able to compete in our future society.

But I have to go and prepare tomorrow's lessons now, excuse me.

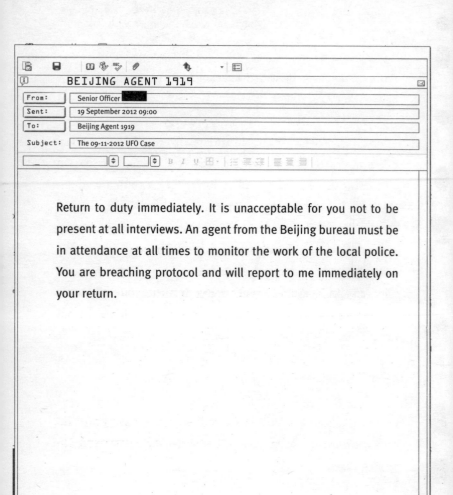

From:	Senior Officer
Sent:	19 September 2012 09:00
To:	Beijing Agent 1919
Subject:	The 09-11-2012 UFO Case

Return to duty immediately. It is unacceptable for you not to be present at all interviews. An agent from the Beijing bureau must be in attendance at all times to monitor the work of the local police. You are breaching protocol and will report to me immediately on your return.

TRANSCRIPT OF INTERVIEW 010
SUBJECT: Kwok Zidong (Old Kwok)
Stall Holder
INTERVIEW DATE: 19 September 2012
AGE: 80
SEX: Male
EDUCATION: Illiterate
POLITICAL STATUS: Peasant
FAMILY STATUS: Widower (wife died 1961);
lives with granddaughter
ADDRESS: Cat Knot Pathway, Silver Hill, House 099
AGENTS PRESENT: Beijing Agent 1919; Hunan Agent 1989

BJ 1919: Right, Grandad, you won't be able to fob me off with stories of noodles, like you did my colleague. It's about time we got to the bottom of all this. I have a feeling people here are hiding things, and if they are, there will be consequences. This chat you supposedly had with butcher Ling Zhu on the morning of 11 September. What was it about? Neither of you has told us.

Chat? With the butcher? I don't remember it.

BJ 1919: You said you went to sleep directly after buying noodles when we know for a fact that, first, you visited the butcher's stall to buy pigs' feet.

Ah, maybe you're right. But what has the butcher got to do with flying plates? I can tell you for a fact, he was no different that day from how he always is – Bitch Bastard gloomy. When you go to his stall, you'll always find him dozing away behind his blood-soaked table with half a pig on it, stomach open, the four feet laid out like chess pieces, a sharp bone-cutting knife planted in the middle, and intestines slithering everywhere. Sometimes he's got a large pig head there. Every fly in Silver Hill gathers around his stall.

After my noodles, I felt like some pigs' feet. My teeth are still good enough to chew on a rubbery pig's foot, and I like sucking the delicious oil from its bones.

The butcher was sleeping. I picked out three feet and weighed them on his rusty scales. The bastard didn't even bother to open his eyes. I calculated the price by myself and was looking for my money when he suddenly groaned: 'Bitch Bastard!'

It made me jump. I thought perhaps I'd done something wrong. And then he grunted, still half asleep:

'There's another one!'

'Another what?'

'Sparrow. See? Where's my gun …'

Oh, no, I begged him not to start with his sparrows again! I've heard that story more than a thousand times. But the bastard went on:

'Cow's Cunt! It's a shame we didn't have more Parasite Eradication Heroes back in the sixties. Then perhaps your wife would still be alive!'

Can you imagine how furious I was? Why did the bastard have to mention my dead wife? What's the point in brooding over all those dreadful events that happened so long ago? I swallowed my words into my heart, took my pigs' feet and went to sit under the Hundred Arm tree. I can tell you, when I want a Bitch Bastard 'chat', I don't go to the butcher.

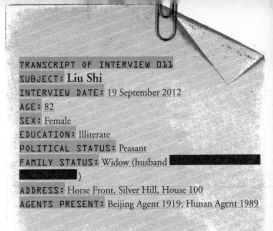

TRANSCRIPT OF INTERVIEW 011
SUBJECT: Liu Shi
INTERVIEW DATE: 19 September 2012
AGE: 82
SEX: Female
EDUCATION: Illiterate
POLITICAL STATUS: Peasant
FAMILY STATUS: Widow (husband ▮▮▮▮▮▮▮▮▮▮
▮▮▮▮▮▮▮)
ADDRESS: Horse Front, Silver Hill, House 100
AGENTS PRESENT: Beijing Agent 1919; Hunan Agent 1989

BJ 1919: What's your name?

HN 1989: Did you hear? He's asking your name.

Did you find my husband then?

BJ 1919: Listen to me, Granny. This is nothing to do with your husband. We need to know your name.

HN 1989: What's your name?

My husband's name is Liu Shengke!

BJ 1919: Dog Sun! Don't get on my nerves. I don't give a damn about your husband. According to your neighbours he died in 1951. That's years before I was born.

Nonsense! You don't know what you're talking about! Typical new generation! Useless! You are from the People's Police, your duty is to serve the people. You have to help me find my husband. Go and ask the People's Liberation Army if my husband is still with them in Tibet. He is a handsome man. He weighs eighty-five kilos – you can imagine how strong he is. He left with them in the spring of 1949, or maybe in 1950, or 1951 … to go and liberate Tibet. Since then, the army has never once given him leave to come and see his wife. Is that normal? Can they keep a husband for ever like that? Every mealtime I put his rice bowl and chopsticks on the table, and I pull up an extra bench, right next to me, for him to sit on if he arrives – his own bench, the one he always sat on. And I talk to that bench. You've got to help me, young man, I am half dead, you can see that for yourselves. This is the only thing I ask from the government before I close my eyes! Help me!

BJ 1919: Granny, stop screaming like that or I'll arrest you. I can't believe I came all the way from Beijing to hear this old hen shriek and moan!

Does your badge there – Beijing 1919 – mean you are from the capital? That's what I thought … You talk like them, with those big words nobody can understand, like on TV for the Party Conference. Can't you talk like everybody else?

BJ 1919: Listen, Granny, I don't have time for your bullshit. I'm only interested in the bloody UFO. You know what I'm talking about, don't you? You told Chief Chang that on 11 September around noon you heard a loud and strange noise near Wong's rice fields.

HN 1989: You just tell the officer what you heard on that day.

I head a very loud noise, young man. And it lasted for a very long time. It was splitting my head. It was Liu Shengke, my husband, calling me from Heaven. I'm sure! Calling me to go and see him! Or maybe I was being cursed. Maybe a curse was being shouted from the Shady Place, telling me to die. But I can't go to the Shady Place, I've got to go to Heaven to find the People's Heroes – to find my husband! I want to leave this world and join him. I am too old. Look at me, young man, I can't walk, my old bones have carried this burden of rotting flesh long enough. But they won't let me die. To die is not so easy, I tell you. I have no teeth left, and with my misty eyes I don't recognise anybody in this village, but I still can't die.

Let me tell you the truth, young man from Beijing. If you don't help me to find my husband in Tibet, I will just die right now in front of your eyes!

BJ 1919: Okay, forget it, I've had enough of her. There's no point in asking her any more questions. She's obviously insane.

HN 1989: That's what I told you before. This woman has been mad for decades. There was never going to be anything to gain from this old granny! You have to trust me, I was born in this province, I know what's in these people's heads.

TRANSCRIPT OF INTERVIEW 012
SUBJECT: Bicycle Mender
          (name unknown)
INTERVIEW DATE: 19 September 2012
AGE: Unknown
SEX: Male
EDUCATION: Unknown
POLITICAL STATUS: Unknown
FAMILY STATUS: Unknown
ADDRESS: Unknown
AGENTS PRESENT: Beijing Agent 1919; Hunan Agent 1989

Beijing Agent 1919: Excuse me for disturbing your work, but do you
know about the UFO that arrived here a few days ago?

?

BJ 1919: Do you understand what I am saying?

?

BJ 1919: You don't understand my Beijing language?

?

BJ 1919: Dog Sun! What a shitty place ... Well, anyway, good luck
with your rusty old fucking bicycles ...

TRANSCRIPT OF INTERVIEW 013
SUBJECT: Zhao Ning
          Secretary to Chief Chang
INTERVIEW DATE: 19 September 2012
AGE: 45
SEX: Male
EDUCATION: Wen Hua Township High School
POLITICAL STATUS: Communist
FAMILY STATUS: Married; no children
ADDRESS: Pine Soil East, Silver Hill, House 036
AGENTS PRESENT: Beijing Agent 1919; Hunan Agent 1989

Comrades, what more can I tell you? I've already noted down all my evidence for Chief Chang. I do not wish to challenge your authority, but when you arrived, you said this investigation would only last for one day and now it's been almost a week and you say your accommodation isn't satisfactory and you want ███████████████

███████████████████████████████████

██████████████████████

Yes, I was there on the afternoon Kwok Yun came running to Chief Chang's office. I think she was a bit scared when she arrived. She had only ever entered the outer office before, where Chief Chang holds meetings for villagers and, on special national occasions, allows them to watch the television. Kwok Yun had never been inside Chief Chang's private office. She kept staring at the pictures of our Great Leaders – Marx, Engels, Lenin, Mao Zedong, Deng Xiaoping – and she was trembling. I don't know if it was because of the UFO she saw, or something else.

When Yun arrived at our office, Chief Chang was reading

the *People's Daily.* I noted down their conversation, thinking it would be useful for our village records. I can give you my transcript, if it would be useful to you.

Document
0002

A record of an important afternoon in Silver Hill by Secretary Zhao

'You won't believe it!' cried Yun as she burst into the room.

Interrupted in her reading, Chief Chang gave Yun a stern look from behind the newspaper.

'Believe what?' she asked in a slightly irritated tone.

'I need to report what I've seen this afternoon!' Yun said.

'Really?' Chief Chang answered without much enthusiasm.

'I was passing Wong's rice fields on my bike when I heard a strange noise in the sky, and then suddenly I saw a big flying plate above my head ...'

Yun was spitting all her words. Chief Chang put down the *People's Daily*, took off her reading glasses and studied her. She seemed to sense that something might really be the matter, so she stood up and poured Yun some Oolong tea.

'Sit down and tell me the whole story from the beginning.'

Yun was trying to catch her breath.

'It was a weird flying metal thing, I tell you! I got such a headache, and I was terrified. It was like being an earthworm and seeing a big bird above you and knowing you're going to get eaten. You know what I mean?'

'Not really,' Chief Chang said soberly. She clearly disapproved of Yun's rough way of speaking.

'What happened next?' Chief Chang asked.

'I don't know. I fainted.'

'What? You fainted? That's hopeless.' Chief Chang's tone became critical. 'How could you just faint like that? I've always thought you were a strong woman.'

'But I started my bleeding today, Chief,' Yun answered in a small voice. Then she carried on with her story:

'When I woke up, that flying thing wasn't there any more.'

Just in case, Chief Chang stood up and peered at the sky through the window, but there was only the boundless blue, not even a cloud. She held her breath and listened for strange sounds from above, but all we could hear were buffaloes lowing in the fields. She returned to her desk, picked up her pen and was about to note down what Yun had said when Yun suddenly spoke again:

'And you know what happened next? I saw a foreigner lying on the grass, a tall foreigner with lots of hairs on his legs!'

At that point, Chief Chang and I realised that the case was serious indeed. Chief Chang pulled out the official buffalo-skin notebook that we use for recording important village events and started to take notes.

'And then? What else did you see?' asked Chief Chang.

'Then I discovered that the foreigner had been bitten by a snake, so I dragged him all the way to my house. There, I washed his wound with sorghum wine, applied a poultice of Yunan powder, and then I bandaged his leg with my grandfather's old shirt.'

Alarmed, Chief Chang had stopped writing.

'You took the foreigner to you house?' she asked.

'Yes, but not by myself, some kids helped. If I hadn't taken him home, he would have died. I bet he was bitten by a "Five-Pace" snake, I promise you, the most poisonous type!'

Chief Chang sipped from her tea, then reprimanded Yun.

'According to the "Foreigners Entering China's Territory" policy, you should have reported the presence of a foreigner to me immediately. You certainly should not have taken him home. In fact, the presence of foreigners in China has never been a private matter, in our whole history! However, in this case, I can understand the urgency. So, what happened after that?'

'Then I made some tea, and went out to fetch some herbs for him. But when I returned, he was gone!'

'Gone where?'

Yun shook her head with a blank face.

Chief Chang seemed worried. 'What did the foreigner look like?' she asked. 'Was he carry anything special, or wearing special attire?'

'He looked … like a man, a little taller than us. He wore a grey T-shirt and a pair of shorts, and he carried only a big bag.'

Chief Chang looked briefly at the calendar on her desk. What she saw there led her to the following conclusion:

'The Beijing International Environment Crisis Conference has recently taken place. It is said that 50,000 international guests attended the meeting. I presume some of those foreigners may have left Beijing and be travelling through China at the moment. Maybe your man is one of the participants. Or a journalist. He might be from the BBC or CNN. That would be a serious matter.'

Chief Chang stared first at Yun, then at me, as if hoping to get some confirmation of what she had just said, but neither of us had anything to add.

'Drink your tea,' ordered Chief Chang. 'It is the best Oolong, from the East Hill region. Hot tea will calm you down.'

Yun swallowed a mouthful of tea. Her eyes started to bulge. It looked as if she had burned her tongue.

'How could these two things vanish without trace?' the Chief muttered to herself.

Then Yun said: 'Today is supposed to be the luckiest day in the Year of the Dragon. I should have left my door open to free the ghosts, but I forgot.'

Chief Chang's face grew dark when she heard this.

'Stop this nonsense at once, Yun! We are living in the twenty-first century! You must rid your mind of all these superstitions and educate yourself to be a modern peasant! A citizen peasant!'

Yun looked embarrassed and fell silent. Chief Chang then picked up the phone and dialled the Town Bureau. She was trying to reach Chu, the head of the Science Department.

Here is what she said:

'Comrade Chu, I need to report a very unusual occurence that took place in Silver Hill today …'

Chief Chang repeated what Yun had said. The conversation

lasted for a long time, maybe around twenty minutes. It wasn't clear what was being said on the other end of the line, but Chief Chang's face grew increasingly serious. When she hung up, she turned to Yun and myself.

'Have you heard of UFOs?' she asked.

'UFwhat?' We had no idea what she was talking about.

'UFOs. Unidentified Flying Objects.'

Yun just stared at her with those big, stupid eyes of hers. Then Chief Chang continued:

'It is thought by some that UFOs carry alien life forms.'

TRANSCRIPT OF INTERVIEW 014
SUBJECT: **Kwok Yun**
INTERVIEW DATE: 20 September 2012
AGE: 37
SEX: Female
EDUCATION: Illiterate
POLITICAL STATUS: Peasant
FAMILY STATUS: Unmarried; lives with grandfather
ADDRESS: Cat Knot Pathway, Silver Hill, House 099
AGENTS PRESENT: Beijing Agent 1919; Hunan Agent 1989

I was very puzzled when Chief Chang mentioned the word 'alien' to me. I didn't understand what she was talking about. All I knew was that the afternoon was unbearably hot and everyone was going to get sunstroke. When Chief Chang ordered me to drink her best Oolong tea, it made me even hotter and I sweated my soul out. The chair I was sitting on got as wet as a sponge. Everyone says that you can only beat the heat by drinking hot tea, well, it has never worked for me. How come everyone believes that? What I needed was a big fridge like the ones on Chief Chang's television. Yes, I wanted to lock myself in a big fridge.

HN 1989: Okay, let's get back to Chief Chang's thoughts about aliens.

Well, when she saw that I didn't know what she was talking about, Chief Chang cleared the table in front of her – telephone, notebooks, pens and papers – and then she brought over the teapot and some cups. She arranged the cups around the pot on the table in a careful shape. They looked so nice that I thought she was going to perform a tea ceremony for me.

'Now look and listen,' she said. 'I'll give you a basic lesson about our Universe. This table is our Universe. The teapot is the sun, hot and burning. My teacup with tea in it is our earth. And these dry, clean cups are the planets around the sun. They have neither water, nor tea leaves. Do you follow me?'

I stared at the clean teacups. I didn't need her to tell me there was no water or Oolong in them. It was obvious. So what?

'But some clever people,' Chief Chang continued, 'believe that far away from this teapot there is another teacup, like mine, that has water and tea in it ... in other words, life. They call the people living there "aliens" and it is possible that these "aliens" can travel across the table from their teacup to ours ...'

Chief Chang poured some hot tea into an empty cup. Instantly the tea leaves swam in all directions in the water.

I stared at the Oolong leaves moving, lurking around like tadpoles. I had a lot of questions:

'If humans live only in your teacup, what are the other teacups for?' I asked.

The certain look on Chief Chang's face went away.

'I can't answer that question,' she said. 'But what I have told you has been proved by Science, for hundreds of years.' When she said the word 'Science', she raised her voice.

I began to feel confused. What did this have to do with

the UFThing? But then Chief Chang explained:

'A UFO doesn't come from our planet. It may be from another world. That's why what you saw is so important. It is the biggest event that could take place in a human life. Do you understand? People will be scared to know this. But I am not scared. Are you?'

I said no, and Chief Chang praised me.

'I don't see what I could be scared of, really,' I said. 'I would be scared if I knew I had nothing to eat tomorrow.' Then I began to worry, because I hadn't yet bought pork for the evening meal.

HN 1989: Tell me, Old Sister, did she make or receive any telephone calls while she was telling you about aliens?

Hmm … you remind me. The telephone did ring. It took her a while to find it because she had moved it from her desk to show me the aliens. When she answered it, Chief Chang's tone was very grave so I guessed it must be some important person. She said things like: 'Yes, I will do', 'Yes, certainly' , 'Yes I will investigate the whole case and report to you tomorrow … ' She had become very modest.

But I was sitting there with millions of urgent questions in my head. I didn't understand one word of what she'd said. As soon as she hung up the phone, I had to ask her about the moon. Could that flying metal plate be from the moon?

'The moon is a satellite. It has no light, no nothing. I don't think aliens could live there,' said Chief Chang.

'What does satellite mean?' I asked.

Chief Chang seemed to be running out of patience with a peasant like me. 'People from the Town Bureau want me to investigate the fields immediately,' she said. 'I have no time for your questions now, but I'm prepared to spend three minutes explaining to you the difference between the planets, satellites and the sun.'

Chief Chang abandoned the teacups on the table and walked towards the blackboard behind me. She found a piece of yellow chalk and began to draw a map.

'See, this is Silver Hill Village. It is a planet. And this is the Town government, which is our sun. Just as the earth receives warmth from circling the sun, so Silver Hill has to circle around the government so we can get financial support, otherwise we would die amidst our tea bushes.'

'But who does the sun circle round?' I asked.

Chief Chang gave me a hard stare

'Who?' she asked. 'I hope you realise that is a political question! We Chinese used to be our own sun, you know. Think of the characters that make up the word China: 中国 – Zhong Guo, a country in the centre of the Universe. We used to stand still, we didn't need to circle around anyone, and others had to circle around China! But unfortunately, in the last century, we were attracted by the Soviet Union, before it fell apart. And now, we are attracted to … no, it's more than attraction, we are actually circling around … the USA.' Chief Chang stopped.

HN 1989: Hang on a second. Did Chief Chang really say we are circling around the USA?

Yes, that's what she said. And she also said America is the sun for the Chinese government.

HN 1989: I'm surprised that a village chief openly says such things in front of a peasant. Anyway, what else did you two speak about?

I was still puzzled by her map, so I asked: 'What about the satellites?'

'You and the other villagers are the satellites,' she said. 'You have no life if you don't spin around the planet which is spinning around the sun. Understand?'

Chief Chang drew many circles around the sun with her yellow chalk. I stared at that messy map and my head began to spin.

And then Chief Chang threw the chalk back into the box, scribbled something in the buffalo-skin notebook, and said, 'Now, finish your tea and come with me. We must go and check Wong's rice fields, and then I'll write my report to the government.'

Although my tongue was still burning from the hot tea, I obediently finished my cup and we left the office.

The last words she said to me that day were:

'Remember, Yun, always use Science to arm your brain, not Superstition.'

HN 1989: And what happened after you made your report to Chief Chang?

I felt very tired so I went home and slept for ever, motionless.

I felt the exhaustion even while I was sleeping, and still the blood kept leaking from my lower body like a quiet river flowing in the night.

When I woke up, the sun was high and the house silent. My grandfather had already gone to the market. Yet again, he hadn't had any breakfast because I hadn't prepared it. I couldn't remember whether I had even seen my grandfather the night before. I had swum in and out of my many dreams, deeply weary from Chief Chang's talk about the universe. I dreamt I was a satellite myself, circling the sun, and then I realised that my body was too heavy to keep circling so it …

HN 1989: Go on …

Well … it's not really worth recording. But as you can see, I am big, I must be as heavy as you. Maybe you think I am even heavier than you … a manly woman, as they say. With that weight, it was impossible for me to keep circling the sun and so my body fell back into complete darkness.

BN 1919: And how did you feel when you woke up?

When I woke from those silly dreams, my ears still echoed with the strange sound from the sky I heard in Wong's fields. I walked into the kitchen and looked hard at the bench, trying to imagine that only yesterday a foreigner with a bleeding leg had sat there. But it felt as if the story of the foreigner was a dream too. There was no trace, nothing unusual in the house.

You might suspect I made it all up, what I saw the other day, but I swear to Heaven, or on the name of Chairman Mao if you prefer, that all I've said is true and I really saw that flying metal plate.

MEMO

From: Beijing Agent 1919
To: Commanding Officer █████
Date: 1 December 2012
Subject: Silver Hill UFO Investigation

I confirm that I have undergone the disciplinary one-month re-education programme at ████████████ and will, in future, obey protocols ████████████ when interviewing subjects.

Further to the findings submitted in September, I would like to add the following comments:

1.   I recommend that Hunan Agent 1989 be put under surveillance. I noticed that, when he spoke to subjects in local dialect, he did not always give me a full translation of what was said. I suspected that he had excessive sympathy for the residents of the village, which would prejudice his findings.

2.   Hunan Agent 1989 has made enquiries into military aerial activity in the vicinity of Silver Hill Village during the first half of September in the belief that Kwok Yun may have mistaken an aeroplane or satellite for a UFO. Having found nothing, he concludes that the metal plate was a figment of her imagination. In my opinion,

this derives from Hunan Agent 1989's overly sympathetic methods. I recommend that we continue to monitor all aerial activity in Hunan Province, nearby Sichuan Province, as well as in Tibet, and visit peasant Kwok Yun on a regular basis.

3.   Further efforts should be made to discover the identity of the visiting foreigner.

4.   I did not have confidence in Chief Chang and recommend close monitoring of her leadership. For example, she assured me that her villagers had followed the One Child Policy, but this was demonstrated to be untrue when we visited many households with more than one child.

FILE
TWO

The Hunan Development Authority
A Survey of Silver Hill

Investigation period:
10–30 September 2013

Surveillance status:
Ongoing

Co-ordinator:
Hunan Finance Officer 8

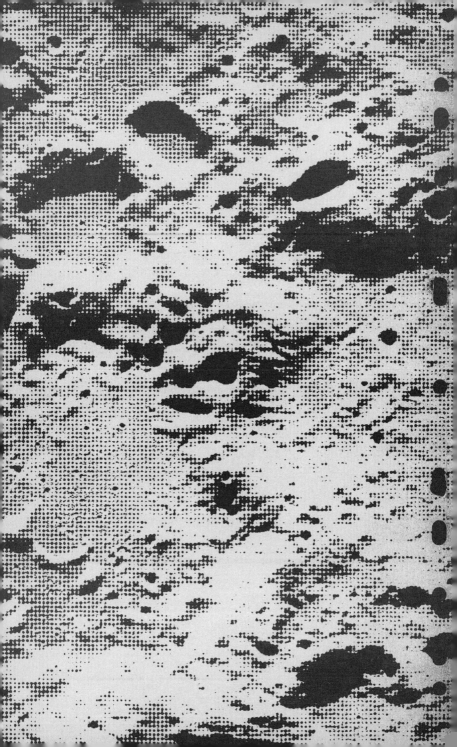

MEMO

From: ▮▮▮▮▮▮▮▮▮
To: Hunan Finance Officer 8
Date: 1 September 2013

TASK:

1.   To check that Silver Hill village is adhering to regulations set out in ▮▮▮▮▮▮▮▮ and will soon be one of China's 'up to speed' villages.

2.   To observe Chief Chang's leadership and confirm that she is the right person to be steering her village into the future.

Enclosed:

1.   Copy of a foreign letter sent to Silver Hill in December 2012

2.   Copy of a letter from village chief, Chang Lee re foreign letter

3.   Copy of report by village secretary Zhao on reception of letter

(Originals held at the National Security and Intelligence Agency – Hunan Bureau)

County Executive's Office
County Road 101
Riverhead
NY 11901
USA

December 25, 2012

Dear Silver Hill villagers,

I imagine you will be surprised to receive a letter like this. I apologize for having to write it in English. Although my stay in your great country inspired me to learn Chinese, I have yet to embark on that ambitious task! I hope that one of you will know enough English to be able to translate it.

Please allow me to introduce myself. My name is Michael Carter and I am the County Executive of Suffolk County, which is in the state of New York, USA. Three months ago, I was hiking through Hunan Province when I got lost in the rice fields and was bitten by a snake. Had it not been for the help of a kind woman who took me to her home and treated the snake bite, I'm sure I would have died. I would like to express my enormous gratitude to this woman. I don't know her name, but she was well built and wearing a red T-shirt sporting the words 'Is This The Future?'. Whoever she was, she is the most generous and courageous person I met during my wonderful trip to China. I thank her from the bottom of my heart, as well as those lovely children who ran to my aid. As a token of my gratitude, I enclose a check for $2000 in the hope that it will help fund your village school and any children in need.

Yours sincerely,

Michael Gorbon

Village Chief's Office
Market Street
Silver Hill

15 February 2013

Dear ████████

Enclosed is a copy of a foreign letter our village has received, together with a Chinese translation by our Headmaster Yee. I ask your permission for us to accept this $2000 cheque. If you have any further questions, don't hesitate to contact me.

I hereby salute you,

张栗
Chief of Silver Hill Village

Reference Document 003

A record of a rather historical event for Silver Hill by Secretary Zhao

Not long before Spring Festival 2013, a very important letter arrived in Silver Hill, sent all the way from the United States of America. Our esteemed Chief Chang saw immediately that it was written in English and so, in a her great wisdom, took it to Headmaster Yee, who is the only person in this village who speaks some English. He took several days to finish his translation, but when he had done so, Chief Chang immediately called a meeting at her office and read the letter to the villagers. After she had finished, the room became like a wok sizzling with stir-fried vegetables. Then everyone suddenly turned to look at Yun, who was standing at the back wearing her foreign T-shirt (ever since she saw the UFO, she wears this red T-shirt on important occasions).

'Headmaster Yee,' said Chief Chang, 'is it correct that the characters on Kwok Yun's T-shirt are in the English language?'

All the villagers' eyes descended to Kwok Yun's chest and she blushed like a beetroot.

'Chief Chang,' Headmaster Yee replied, 'it is correct.'

'And can you tell us, Headmaster Yee, what these characters mean,' our leader continued.

Headmaster Yee thought for a moment. He looked even harder at Kwok Yun's chest, as if he were shortsighted, and then he gave his translation.

'"Is This The Future?"' he said. 'That is what they mean.'

A murmur went round the room. 'Why would anybody write something like that on a shirt?' the villagers whispered. But despite their confusion, they were relieved to know that the foreigner who had appeared in Wong's rice fields was actually a real man, and had not landed in a UFO. Ever since September, the village has been unsettled by the thought that there might be aliens among us.

Folding the precious letter back into its envelope and laying the 2000-dollar cheque on the table for all to see, Chief Chang called for Kwok Yun to come to the front:

'As you will all expect, I have already thoroughly investigated this matter. There is no doubt about it. The woman who saved our American friend is Kwok Yun. Let us applaud her!'

Chief Chang started clapping, and immediately the whole room erupted into loud applause. Only Old Kwok didn't clap. I think he found it hard to follow what was happening, and he was confused – as, in my view, he always is.

Chief Chang then spoke again. I took down her words in the official buffalo-skin notebook:

'I feel very proud of Silver Hill and of Yun's courage. We know from our village records that, previously, we have only ever had one visit from the USA, and that was sixty years ago, from an American journalist who was writing an article to introduce the greatness of our Chairman Mao to the West. This new link with America will, I am sure, have a great impact on Silver Hill, and will benefit our village in the future. I am glad that we have such a good Citizen Peasant as Kwok Yun among us!'

Of course Yun blushed deeply and lowered her head.

No one in the village had ever seen a cheque before. Fu Qiang – 'Rich and Strong' – rose from his seat, agitated, and grabbed it. 'Bitch Bastard!' he swore – he was impressed. He started to study the English writing on the cheque with much curiosity, while the others crowded round behind him, trying to catch a glimpse.

'You mean that little piece of paper is going to give us 2000 dollars?' one peasant asked. 'How do you know that?'

'You idiot!' said Rich and Strong. 'Of course we trust Americans! If they say it's 2000 then 2000 Bitch Bastard dollars it is.'

When he said this, an argument broke out in the room.

'You think you're so clever Rich and Strong, but you're not. Look at that messy writing on it. No trader is going to accept that!'

Chief Chang tried to calm them down: 'This is a cheque. It is a sort of civilised money, based on human trust.'

Then everyone started to discuss why Silver Hill couldn't have that kind of civilised paper money too, until Rich and Strong interrupted by asking how much 2000 dollars was in Chinese currency. Chief Chang found a wooden abacus in her drawer and started moving the beads about. In no time she had an answer: 'According to the exchange rate I found in the *People's Daily* last week, it is about 6850 yuan.' When we heard the figure, everybody got excited and the room became very noisy.

Headmaster Yee is a respectful man with good manners, but even he couldn't help raising his voice.

'It seems to me,' he shouted, 'that Mr Michael Carter made it clear in the letter that this money is to be given to the school. I hope everyone remembers that as well as I do. 6850 yuan, that's half a year's budget for our school!'

Rice-grower Wong was trying to say something, but Rich and Strong interrupted him. 'What about us?' he argued. 'What about the families whose children have already left school?'

Chief Chang gave Rich and Strong a disdainful look. Everyone knows that Rich and Strong's son has a good job in the city, working in a bank. He should be grateful for the help Headmaster Yee gave his family. 'Listen,' she said, 'this foreign help arrives at a time when our village desperately needs it! Education is the first and foremost thing Silver Hill needs. The cheque will be turned into cash and then sent to the school without delay.'

I think this made Headmaster Yee very happy. He's the most devoted teacher you can imagine, and he has been struggling a lot with the school budget. I saw him thanking Yun again and again, shaking her hand and telling her how much the village had benefited from her kindness to the foreigner.

After a moment, Chief Chang cleared her throat and

made another official announcement:

'As you probably all know, each year the Town Government awards a medal for the most progressive peasant. I'm proud to announce that this year's "Model Peasant" medal has been awarded to Kwok Yun. She lost her parents when she was a baby, but she manages to fight back, beat the hardships and live as an independent woman. On top of that, Yun has been responsible for the two most important events in our village's history: the sighting of a real UFO, and the rescuing of an important American. Everyone should learn from Yun's positive spirit!'

When Chief Chang hung the medal on Yun's neck, I watched Yun carefully to see her reaction. She looked excited, but she didn't smile. She is like a frog, she never smiles.

'For the last thirty years,' Chief Chang said, raising her hand to show everyone she was going to make an important speech, 'the people of Silver Hill have eaten enough bitterness to last us to eternity! And because we are poor and uneducated, we have been unaware of what has been going on in the rest of our country, let alone in the world! Well, I can tell you that, recently, China has changed beyond recognition. Silver Hill is running far behind. It is time for us to do something!'

Chief Chang's tone got more and more fiery. She stared at Yun, who was standing in front of her. 'We need to progress quickly, but how?'

'How?' parroted Yun, in a frightened tone.

'Let me tell you how!' thundered Chief Chang. 'By grabbing the opportunities that present themselves.

By creating business connections. And now, these opportunities and connections have arrived: a UFO and a Westerner. We have the chance to catch up! As our important philosopher Wang Chong said 2000 years ago, sky and earth are in harmony, therefore the great force can come now. I am going to make a reform plan and ask for support from the government.'

What a mighty woman our Chief Chang is. We all left that meeting with our heads full of America, dollars, medals, and Chief Chang's upbeat words.

ID Card No: 338145365445889
Interviewer: Hunan Finance Officer 8
Date: 10 September 2013

HFO 8: Eight months ago, yourself and Chief Chang wrote to us to request financial support for the improvement of Silver Hill. As a result, the province authorities have released two million yuan to improve the village's living conditions. I've come here to monitor and assess the development of the region.

Welcome, Comrade. It's good to see you, especially at a time when our village is in such good shape.

But I'm actually quite busy this morning: I have to prepare for Chief Chang's meeting this afternoon with the head of a plastics factory from Changsha. He is thinking of setting up a subsidiary here. Can I just give you a quick overview of Silver Hill's development?

1. We are making substantial improvements to our infrastructure – building new roads, a sewage system and so on. (But you'll have to ask Chief Chang directly about these large-scale plans: I wouldn't want to give you wrong information.)

2. We have bought twenty Legend computers and

opened a 'Future Technology Hub'. We have also started a free 'walk-in' peasant training centre, so they can learn how to read and write.

3.   With the money the village has been able to set aside to support education, nearly every child can now go to school and study without worrying about paying the fees.

4.   Twice a week, we hold a 'walk-in-college' for the villagers, at which Chief Chang introduces current affairs and subjects of interest that she reads about in the newspapers.

5.   We have also opened an 'Old People's Palace' in the main street, next to the market. Since most of our villagers are elderly, we decided we should provide them with a centre where they can go to entertain themselves and feel part of a community. We provide games like chess, go and poker, TV, tea, pumpkin seeds and so forth.

HFO 8: I hear that a successful businessman from Canton came to give a lecture here last week. Can you tell me about that?

Yes, we were very fortunate that the famous Huang Lingdong chose to pay a visit to our village and to give us his 'Make Yourself Rich' lecture. He had heard about the UFO and wanted to see Wong's remarkable rice field for himself.

The lecture took place in Chief Chang's meeting room. There were two reasons, she said, why Huang Lingdong had become such a significant public figure in south China:

1.   He is a millionaire and owns a huge factory making electricity generators etc. He even has his own private helicopter.

2.   A few years ago, he made a name for himself in the literary world by publishing *The Path to Being a Millionaire*. In that book he explains how he made his fortune in Shenzhen by teaching what he called 'Ltd English', the 200 words you need to do business with foreigners. The book also described his remarkable journey from pig farmer to BMW-driving millonaire, from village hovel to Shenzhen mansion.

The lecture was very interesting. Although, to tell you the truth, I think it went a little over the heads of some of the villagers. None of them had ever heard of Huang Lingdong before. But perhaps that's not so surprising: although our villagers are not stupid, they rarely read books or papers, and only very few own a TV. How could they be expected to know that some millionaire had written a book, or what 'Ltd English' is? And anyway, there are so many millionaires in Canton and Shenzhen that it's hard to keep up with them: anybody talking on a mobile phone or coughing in a Canton street might be a millionaire. China is big, life is not equal, and nothing is fair.

So, to get back to the lecture. All through it, Huang clutched his book, soaked in his sweat, and waved it at the audience to emphasise his words.

'There are ten rules to follow if you want to become a millionaire,' he said. 'If you follow them faithfully, I promise you will leave behind this – to say the least – very mediocre situation you are in now …'

I wrote down his rules in my notebook. Let me read to you what he said:

'The first two rules are philosophical. To have a millionaire's

mind, you must train yourself to think as follows:

1. I will not let life decide for me: I can create my life with my own two hands.

2. There is no destiny or fate in life, there is only strong will, and that will is my destiny.

The remaining rules are practical:

1. Get a US dollar credit card for online purchasing. The corollary to this rule is that you'll also have to learn how to use the internet.

2. Never invest your own money. You have to use or borrow other people's money first. So you don't hurt your own life if things go wrong.

3. Always buy the cheapest products, including recycled rubbish. Process it, beautify it and repackage it, then sell it at a high price.

4. ...

I stopped at 'rule six' because I had to go and make some Oolong tea for him and Chief Chang, who was listening to the lecture in the front row.

Obviously, the subject was important to everyone, but the millionaire spoke in such a strange dialect (I presume from some village in Canton Province), and it was such a hot afternoon that his dull voice soon sent everyone to sleep.

After the lecture, Chief Chang announced that the subject of the following week's 'walk-in college' would be a discussion of the comparative virtues of American and Japanese harvesting machines. By then, the millionaire seemed in a hurry to leave and he excused himself, saying that he had to be in the city in the evening for an important business banquet. His BMW was waiting outside in the scorching sun.

As he left with his leather briefcase, waving his hand like the Japanese film star Ken Takakura from *Yellow Handkerchief of Happiness*, he said, 'Good luck everyone! Remember my ten rules, and maybe one day you too will own a helicopter. And by the way, you can buy my "Ltd English" textbook in any bookshop. The price is lower now, only thirty-five yuan including two CDs. Also, my factory, Western Power, makes all sorts of power generators and boilers, from gas to coal-burning, from diesel-powered to hydroelectric, so if you need any of these you can call 0813 8888888 and I will give you a discount. Goodbye!'

So that was it. With black smoke escaping from the back of his BMW, the best-selling boilermaker left us for his big city.

ID Card No: 331643343886009
Interviewer: Hunan Finance Officer 8
Date: 10 September 2013

HFO 8: Hello, Chief Chang. You know the reason why I'm here, don't you?

Of course. My secretary informed me of your visit. Please take a seat and I'll make you some tea. As you can see, my office has become less spacious because of the new computer and furniture, but do find a sofa you feel comfortable in. I've got some very good Oolong here.

HFO 8: Thank you. It seems that you and your team are in good spirits.

Indeed. Here is your tea. Be careful, it's hot.

First, I want you to record my official and sincere gratitude for the Provincial Government's support. After the famous UFO event, I am proud to say that our village is developing at an impressive rate. You can now see fridges and TV sets in most households. Many peasants have started to read newspapers, and they can tell you where Switzerland is, or the state of Utah. Younger ones are learning how to use computers and are ambitious to open new businesses. That's why I am asking your authority for further help.

Comrade, the project I'm most proud of is of course the tourism centre which we're building on the spot where the UFO appeared. The site, a rice field, is still in the early stages of development but we have already erected a monument to the UFO: a marble sculpture shaped like a saucer. In the coming months, we plan to open a café and a history museum. That part of Silver Hill will become a major tourist attraction.

In order to make sure we meet all our goals, we have drawn up a detailed Five Year Plan, which is written here on my board. Please let me read it to you:

2013–2018 Five Year Plan – Region of Silver Hill

By the end of 2018, we aim to have achieved the following:

1. The completion of a highway which will connect Silver Hill to the cities of Changsha and Heng Yang in only fifteen minutes.

2. The construction of a forty-mile canal creating a water link between the Yangtze River and Dongting Lake. This will allow us to renovate Silver Hill's irrigation system, and will attract freshwater fishing industries as well as leisure boats.

3. The transformation of large sections of agricultural land into industrial zones, and the recruitment of a large labour force for the manufacturing firms that bring their businesses here. (We will need several banks in order to exchange foreign currency into yuan and to provide that most important of services: the credit card.)

4. To make Silver Hill a city with modern facilities including theatres, cinemas, hotels, tennis courts, golf courses, colleges and a swimming pool. In short, a civilised environment. By 2018 our villagers will have become modern citizens, able to enjoy a modern lifestyle and culture.

Allow me to show you a map, laying out what the new Silver Hill might look like.

As you will see, this map has been created on my new Legend computer, using the latest town-planning software kindly provided by your head office: Town Fantastic 1.3. My new computer has allowed me to revolutionise the organisation of my office. No more telephone and filing cabinets! No more buffalo-skin notebooks! We have become fully digital.

For map see reference document 004

SILVER HILL CITY IN 2018

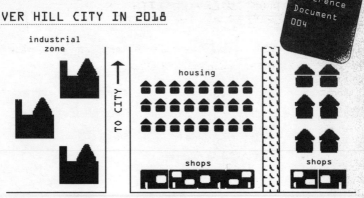

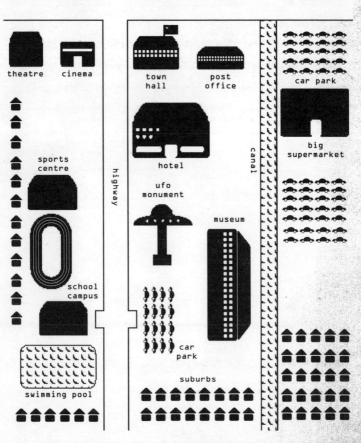

industrial zone

TO CITY

housing

shops

shops

theatre

cinema

town hall

post office

car park

sports centre

hotel

big supermarket

highway

ufo monument

museum

canal

school campus

car park

swimming pool

suburbs

TRANSCRIPT OF INTERVIEW WITH
BICYCLE REPAIRER AT THE MARKET

ID Card No: Unable to produce ID card at time of interview
Interviewer: Hunan Finance Officer 8
Date: 11 September 2013

HFO 8: Sorry to stop your work for a minute, but I would like to conduct some interviews in this market. As a peasant in this village, what do you think of Chief Chang's special Five Year Plan?

?

HFO 8: Have you not heard of the new Five Year Plan that will be implemented in this region?

?

HFO 8: You aren't local?

?

HFO 8: OK, let's try using Beijing language ...

Sorry, I am only a bike mender.

TRANSCRIPT OF INTERVIEW WITH FU QIANG

ID Card No: 335656787856772
Interviewer: Hunan Finance Officer 8
Date: 11 September 2013

HFO 8: Is your name Fu Qiang?

Yes, but they call me Rich and Strong. Don't you think that's a better name?

HFO 8: I can see the point. So you are a tea farmer, is that right?

Well, you could say that. I have those tea bushes up on the hill, but these days I'm more interested in Chief Chang's Five Year Plan. 'Five Year Plan'! You know, the second I heard those words, the blood rushed to my head. Bitch Bastard, I thought, Silver Hill is finally going to make some noise in the world! Perhaps we'll have the chance to get rich at last, like all those people in Shanghai. My son's there. I don't hear from him much and he never visits me. Wants to forget all about Silver Hill. I don't blame him, but if I had a bit of money I could go to Shanghai to visit him.

Bitch Bastard, I hope this Five Year Plan of Chief Chang's works out. You see, Officer, we old people remember the Five Year Plan in the fifties. And that was quite something, Bitch

Bastard! We were catching up with Soviet and American Imperialism! But it didn't end well. Okay, at the beginning the result was better harvests, but later it turned into the largest Bitch Bastard disaster we had ever seen: the Great Famine. So you ask me what I think of another Five Year Plan? Well, I'll tell you. It's shit scary. But I don't want to be reactionary. Besides, I'm a peasant, I don't even own my tea fields. The State owns everything, including my life. So I'm ready to try again. Times have changed, everybody in China is getting rich, why not Silver Hill? And why not me?

HFO 8: Do you think Chief Chang is a good leader?

Oh yes. You know, when we went to Chief Chang's office to hear about her great Five Year Plan, instead of giving us Oolong tea as usual, she opened a bottle of Maotai wine and gave everyone a sip. 'Bitch Bastard!' I thought. 'That bottle must have cost 2000 yuan. Isn't Maotai only for top officials, or for when you want to bribe someone? What's she doing serving it to us?' But I didn't argue. I knocked it back and, Bitch Bastard, it was delicious! I bet official people like you get a chance to drink it all the time.

HFO 8: Not all the time. Everybody knows that Maotai wine distribution is reserved for foreign diplomats, for US, Russian or French presidents when they visit China. You may remember that it was the wine Chairman Mao drank with Richard Nixon during their state banquet. But I have to warn you that we officials don't accept bribes. We are not interested in that, you understand?

ID Card No: 334565334229008
Interviewer: Hunan Finance Officer 8
Date: 11 September 2013

HFO 8: Sorry to stop your work, but I need to ask you a few questions. It won't take long. Is that okay?

Who are you? You are stepping on my rice plants. Move your feet.

HFO 8: I have been appointed by the Hunan Development Authority to oversee your village's economic reform. I imagine you are the owner of this field?

Yes, this is my rice field. I say again, you are stepping on my crops!

HFO 8: Sorry about that. I didn't notice them.

You can step on this bit of grass if you want. I see you don't know the difference between weeds and crops.

HFO 8: Well, I am not a peasant like you, and therefore not an agricultural expert. If you want to know, I have an MA in International Business Studies. Anyway, leaving qualifications to one side – do you know about the future plans for Silver Hill?

Future? Are you asking about that flying plate again?

HFO 8: No, I'm here to investigate a different matter. It is about your village's improvement.

You call it improvement? To tell you the truth, I can't see anything improving about it. What have they got planned for my rice fields, that's what I want to know. Have you seen that Bitch Bastard monument they've already put on my land? My kid read me what's written on that stupid marble dish:

> On 11 September 2012, on this spot, Model
> Peasant Kwok Yun sighted a UFO, thus making
> a significant contribution to science.

Can you believe it? It doesn't even mention my name! This is my rice field, no one else's! They just appeared one day with trucks and cement, trashed my whole field with their stupid bulldozer, and in no time they put up that thing. Bitch Bastard! When I asked Chief Chang how she was planning to compensate me, all she had to say was: 'As the event happened in your field, the new, modern Silver Hill will be forever grateful and proud of you.'

Can you believe I had to listen to that rubbish? So what I

say is, I'll shut my mouth if her Five Year Plan ends up doing me some good. But for now, I'll just keep on counting and counting again how much money I've lost, money which was going to pay for my children's future. You hear me?

ID Card No: 331643343886009
Interviewer: Hunan Finance Officer 8
Date: 12 September 2013

HFO 8: Chief Chang, I have heard different points of view from your villagers about the Five Year Plan. How do you yourself view it?

Well, of course a democratic country ought to allow different views, but I'm sure our villagers will come to understand that this is the best way. There is already a noticeable change in their ways of thinking. Although it seems unlikely that they will all become millionaires like best-selling Huang – nobody can speak even 'Ltd English' here – our people are starting to open their minds to other kinds of life. This is very unusual and new. Historically, the peasant's lifestyle has been communist: each peasant would diligently follow the precepts set out by Chairman Mao in his Little Red Book. There was no need for individual opinions or desires: the only options were to join the army or to grow rice, and no one tried to do anything else. All this worked in those days. But now, Comrade, I am sure you'll agree with me that we in Silver Hill need to adapt to a new economic environment. I am confident that, if the other villages of China have been able to turn themselves into major international industrial centres, so can we.

ID Card No: 338145365445889
Interviewer: Hunan Finance Officer 8
Date: 12 September 2013

HFO 8: Secretary Zhao, as you work very closely with the village chief, is there anything you'd like to add to Chief Chang's comments?

You will see, Comrade, this is going to be the biggest time for Silver Hill! Even now we are currently creating an even more detailed map with Town Fantastic 1.3, showing how the highway linking us to cities in the north and south will cut through the hills. Tunnels have to be dug, bridges built. A great project indeed, and one I am confident we can achieve in five years. In the process, the old must make way for the new.

'Demolish the weak, demolish the rotten!' I'm sure you will have seen these slogans painted up on the walls around here. Old houses are being torn down, new buildings put in their place. We are doing all this in consultation with a team of experts from a private development company. The building works are about to start, and already trucks are bringing cement and steel. Construction workers are arriving –

migrant labourers from all over China. You won't recognise our streets. Before, the only stranger in our midst was the bicycle mender at the market. Now our village is filled with unfamiliar workers, wearing yellow helmets and speaking different dialects. At first the villagers were confused by the line of brick sheds going up near the rice fields. They wanted to know who the dwellings were for. But then they realised that, before doing anything, the construction workers had to build their own housing: 'It will be a long time before we leave here,' the workers explained, 'so we must first build our accommodation!' Anyone with a brain can understand that we must share our village if we are going to build the future together. Don't you think so, Comrade?

HFO 8: I am here to listen to your answers, not to provide answers of my own. Tell me about Chief Chang. Do you believe she has the strength of character to lead the village through this great change?

I can tell you straight away, she is a great woman. In my whole life I have not met a woman as intelligent and serious as her. You should study her face carefully: she may be fifty-three, but she is full of energy; her high cheekbones and big earlobes show her unerring certainty.

And you must also consider her army background, and the famous medal story, which everyone around here knows. It was awarded to her father for his heroic behaviour during the Korean War against America in 1951, when our army fought on the side of North Korea: standing together to resist American Imperialism! Internationalism, that's what we call it! You know that a million Chinese people died in that war and only 50,000 American soldiers, but even so the Americans eventually lost.

Chief Chang's mother also worked for the army, she was a nurse. Therefore Chief Chang was specially looked after by the Communist Party and sent to study in an Army College in the seventies: she specialised in hybrid plants. She is definitely one of the most knowledgeable people in the region. 'Poverty causes trouble, knowledge is the way,' she often says to me. She has herself eaten much bitterness. You can read that in her frown and her wrinkles. But her past sadness inspires her to do great things. She dedicates her whole life to work, unlike that weak husband of hers. While he mopes around, she studies by herself in the office after everyone has gone home. 'We must "convert sorrow into strength" as our party encourages us to do,' she tells me. This is why she wants me to create a village museum, to show our villagers the difficulties we have suffered through history, and how important it is that we become strong and resolute. Indeed, whenever Chief Chang gives a speech, everybody is confident that she is only doing what is best for Silver Hill and that, under her leadership, no villager will ever again starve to death.

Minutes of the Silver Hill Village Meeting 13 September 2013

Taken by Secretary Zhao

ITEM 1 Socialism.

'What is socialism and what is Marxism?' asked Chief Chang, reading from Deng Xiaoping's Collected Speeches. As Deng Xiaoping said in a famous speech in the eighties, "Poverty is not socialism". In the past, the true definition of socialism was not clear. Now, we can see that if socialism is the primary stage of communism leading to the advanced stage where the principle "from each according to his ability and to each according to his needs" can be applied, then the fundamental task for socialism is to develop the productive forces to a level where there is an overwhelming abundance of material wealth. The superiority of the socialist system to the capitalist system will be demonstrated by its ability to develop those forces faster and better. As they develop, the people's material and cultural life will consistently improve. Socialism means eliminating poverty.'

'What is Democracy?' asked Chief Chang, reading from the People's Daily. 'Some people think Democracy means everybody can do whatever they want. Not at all! Democracy means that the government collects opinions and thoughts from the citizens in order to develop better plans for the nation. Chinese Democracy is different from the Democracies of Western countries, in particular America. American Democracy is just an excuse for invading other countries and destroying nations, for example Iraq. It is used to bully and exploit other countries. This kind of Democracy is a political game, a dangerous concept, and it can cause great trouble. We will continue to study this at the next village meeting.'

Chief Chang informed the meeting that a tennis court would be built next to Carp Li's fish pond, since the land in that area is flat. She then gave the following speech:

'What does Silver Hill have that big cities don't? Natural resources! In other words, mountains, fields, ponds – space! We should use our space as a source of income. A tennis court will attract city people to come and enjoy our beautiful natural resources. On the basis of this, we will be able to build a sport and leisure industry.

ID Card No: 331248672238784
Interviewer: Hunan Finance Officer 8
Date: 13 September 2013

HFO 8: Excuse me, could I take a moment of your time? I believe you are Model Peasant Kwok Yun, the woman who saw the UFO?

Yes.

HFo 8: May I ask how old you are.

I am thirty-eight this year.

HFO 8: And do you always attend Chief Chang's meetings?

Always. After I became a Model Peasant, Chief Chang told me I had to educate myself, so I come here every week.

HFo 8: Chief Chang tells me you also have private lessons with Headmaster Yee.

Yes, I go to the school every Sunday. At first it was difficult to go there on the right day. In the village, we live according to the Chinese calendar. Only the school uses the Western system. We never think that we are picking our tea on a Monday or a Wednesday, we only pick it because it is ready on that day. So anyway, doing something on a Sunday made me nervous. I had to check the calendar to find out whether it was Sunday or not. Also I thought it was too late for me to learn – I could never become like Huang the millionaire who knows how to do internet purchases with his American credit card.

But I have to admit, the headmaster has given me some knowledge.

HFO 8: Like what?

A bit of writing, geography, maths. I am not as good at maths as others. I'm not clever, I'm sure you can see that. For example, minus numbers. Headmaster Yee says that $3 - 4 = -1$. But what is this -1? Is it a real thing?

I think I am really stupid – a stupid peasant who doesn't understand that minus can be very useful for the community.

HFO 8: Certainly, minus is very important in the process of development. If you study an economic chart, you'll find out that if there is no minus, there can't be a plus either. But tell me. Because of your kindness to a foreigner, the school has received additional resources. Have they made a difference?

Oh yes. Headmaster Yee has worked diligently to build up

the school. I remember the goals on the football pitch outside the window, they used to be made out of rope slung between two bamboo sticks. And pupils didn't have any pens then. Now, they have proper goalposts, some wooden Ping Pong tables and they all have pens and books.

HFO 8: So do you think the school now has enough resources?

Well … I think Headmaster Yee needs help. He works so hard he even sleeps at the school, on a bed under the blackboard. He says that he doesn't have time to look for a wife, and that even if he had one, he wouldn't have time to look after her.

HFO 8: Perhaps you could help him?

Me? What do I know about children? … You know, I always find it strange to be in a school, as I have no connection to kids. Sometimes I wonder, what is it like to have children? Does it hurt when they are ashamed of you for being ugly and stupid? Does it make you sad when the day comes for them to go to the big city?

I should stop this nonsense. It's not useful to you …

ID Card No: 334345239004934
Interviewer: Hunan Finance Officer 8
Date: 14 September 2013

HFO 8: Please confirm to me that your name is Li Sheng.

No use calling me that. If you ask people around here for someone of that name, no one will know who you are talking about. Carp Li is what they call me, because I raise and sell carp fish. But of course there is more than just carp in my pond: I have shrimps, catfish, crabs, tilapias. You should try my carp, it tastes better than the fish from any other pond. And you know why? I'll tell you: because no chemicals or pesticides end up in my pond. You might think my water looks a bit muddy, but I tell you, that's how it should be. My water is the cleanest there is.

HFO 8: I will take a look at your carp when I leave. But I have more serious issues to discuss with you. I presume you have heard about the tennis court that is to be built here?

Hell! Is it you that's responsible for this Bitch Bastard tennis court?

HFO 8: No, I come from Changsha. I am simply monitoring the development of your village.

Well, why did they have to send you? Why couldn't they tell me about it directly? Of course I know about this shit. A few days ago some official people came to my pond and stirred it up with their measuring rods. And then this morning they dumped a load of sand and bricks on my land. But I've never been asked to attend those meetings at Chief Chang's office. Maybe they think I am a stupid shrimp who doesn't understand anything. If you want to know the truth, I don't like what the village authority is doing. I also heard in the wind that the canal they want to build will go through my pond. You're the expert, so you tell me: if that happens, will my pond still belong to me?

HFO 8: I'm afraid it's not my role to answer your questions.

And if my pond becomes part of some state canal, what about my fish? Will any old bastard in any bastard place be able to catch my fish?

HFO 8: I am afraid I can't help you. I am merely gathering information.

Those Communists! I am not talking about you, Comrade, I am talking about the people who do things only gangsters would do. I know gangsters very well, I nearly became one when I was young. And don't tell me I am reactionary. They will steal my pond! I'll tell you what: in Silver Hill, there's only one clever person, and that's Headmaster Yee. 'Don't worry so much,' he told me. 'You know carp are a highly invasive species, they'll spread wherever there is fresh water. They can leap over cliffs and jump to different waters to reproduce. So in the end, you'll probably end up with more fish.'

Those are the words of an educated man. And it's true, carp are good at leaping, I know it. But who says those carp will only leap into my pond, and not away into somebody else's?

Anyway, you tell me why Silver Hill needs some useless tennis court, and why we need a canal. What for? So that people can hit balls about and pretend to be Western, or float down the water in pleasure boats listening to flute players and warblers like the emperors and their concubines used to do thousand of years ago?

HFO 8: I can only speak about China's current situation. If one wants to stand tall and to cast a great shadow, one has to clear a space around oneself first. Surely you can understand that. One single person's business will not grow strong unless the whole area is getting rich. As our Chinese aphorism says: *bu she bu de* – no discard, no gain.

I understand nothing of what you're saying.

But who cares whether an illiterate peasant like me understands or not anyway? Don't waste your time on me, young man, go and talk to some sensible people.

TRANSCRIPT OF INTERVIEW WITH KWOK ZIDONG

ID Card No: 338768742234441
Interviewer: Hunan Finance Officer 8
Date: 15 September 2013

HFO 8: Tell me your name and status.

Everyone in this area knows who I am. I am Old Kwok, I run a 'five metals' stall in the market, and I am the grandfather of Yun – the 'UFO Witness' as you city people would say.

HFO 8: Thank you, Grandpa. We in Changsha have heard a lot about your granddaughter. She is famous. Anyway, I am here for a different matter. Have you heard your village is building a tennis court by Carp Li's pond?

Which Bitch Bastard has made that stupid decision? Carp Li is my best friend, and I can see this business is driving him mad.

HFO 8: What do you mean 'driving him mad'?

I saw him yesterday morning. He was fishing for crabs. He caught two little buckets of Blue Crab, and then he told me something odd:

'All my crabs have gone to Europe!' he said with his eyes fixed on the water. I didn't pay much attention – I thought he must be drunk. But he kept going on about it.

'Yes, my crabs have gone to the West, for real! Didn't you listen to the radio this morning? They said some English people found lots of Blue Crabs in their river, or maybe in their sea, and then some scientists studied those crabs and found out they actually swam from China. I'm sure some of them are my crabs. My crabs are good swimmers …'

When I heard that, I murmured to myself, 'What the hell is he talking about? There is no bastard sea around here. How could those crabs swim away from Silver Hill, when we ourselves have never even managed to move to the next village? Is he losing his mind?'

Anyway, he continued to ramble on about his crabs but I stopped listening. At that point, a Bitch Bastard monster truck arrived in front of us, and started pouring tons of sand on to the ground, spilling it into Carp Li's pond. Then another one, carrying a load of bricks, parked nearby. 'What a mess,' I thought. 'What's going on here?'

Then Carp Li spoke bitter words, words that hurt me:

'Let's all say a big thank you to your granddaughter, and her flying plate. Look at this place! Soon it will look like Hong Kong, and we'll all lose our livelihoods. I can't read, I can't write and I can't drive. What am I going to do? And they won't let me keep my pond, you can bet your last Bitch Bastard yuan on that! Look at those trucks! Look at my pond now!'

HFO 8: How much did he know about the plans for the village's development?

A hell of a lot more than you think, young man. You may believe that his mind is as knotted as mine, but I can tell you: he knew everything.

'They can't take your pond away!' I said to him. 'They know the whole of Silver Hill needs to buy your fish.'

He looked at me as if I was an idiot: 'Your brain is as Bitch Bastard old as those rotten Hundred Arm trees!' he said. 'Don't you know they are building a supermarket?'

'A supermarket?' I had never heard of such a thing.

'A supermarket is a huge bastard shop with a roof, where they sell everything: rice cookers, flour, salt, kettles, beds, TV sets, lights, washing machines, clothes, hammers, nails ...'

When he said hammers and nails, I began to shit my pants.

'Yes,' he said, looking hard at me. 'A supermarket sells everything you can find on your shabby little "five metals" stall – and more! You'll lose all your customers.'

When I heard that, I nearly lost my Bitch Bastard mind. How will I survive if no one buys their tools from me? And then I thought, well, I have lived long enough, but what about my granddaughter? She's still young. How will she support herself? Since she became a Model Peasant, Chief Chang has been sending her to school, but what use is number-learning if you have nothing to sell? To tell the truth, I am against all this education business. It won't find her a husband,

and I have to work harder because she doesn't have time to help me.

'What is more,' Carp Li continued, 'if there is a supermarket, they will put foreign fish and foreign shrimps on its Bitch Bastard shelves!'

A foreign shrimp in Silver Hill! Bitch Bastard! I tried to get my head round the idea. A foreign shrimp in Silver Hill ... I am too old. Soon my eyes will be shut and the Shady Place will take me, and these wretched things won't matter any more.

ID Card No:	3345567355698887
Interviewer:	Hunan Finance Officer 8
Date:	15 September 2013

HFO 8: Are you Ling the butcher?

Of course I'm the butcher, Cow's Cunt! You have eyes, you can see my pork under your nose.

HFO 8: Does your family run the business with you?

No, I don't let anyone else touch my business. What do you want?

HFO 8: Butcher, let's get straight to the point. The Food Hygiene Office has informed us that your meat stall does not meet the standards of cleanliness required to be allowed to sell food to the public.

Food Hygiene Office? Cow's Cunt! I've been living in Silver Hill for more than sixty years and I've never heard of such a thing! I couldn't give a dog's arse what any Food Hygiene Office says.

HFO 8: Be careful of what you say, Butcher. I've come all the way from the provincial capital Changsha to monitor your village's progress. All my interviews will be passed back to the Development Authority. It's a part of our job to help you improve your business. It is your job to act on our recommendations.

Well, you can see for yourself how many flies and mosquitoes there are in this rotten village. How do you expect me to stop them?

HFO 8: Here is a leaflet about food hygiene, setting out the responsibility of the Food Hygiene Office to protect the people's health, and to maintain food standards. If you consult page three you will find information about fly management. I suggest you read it carefully. The number of flies on your pork is unacceptable.

Too many flies on my pork? Well, I'll kill them then. I don't need any leaflet to tell me that. And besides, I can't read. No problem for me to kill flies. As I'm sure you know, I'm a Parasite Eradication Hero.

HFO 8: Yes, we know about that. But it certainly doesn't make you a man with good habits. What you have to do is get a fridge in which to store your pork, otherwise you won't be allowed to sell it any more. Your business certificate will be taken from you until you have a fridge.

I can't believe what I'm hearing! Cow's Cunt! How dare you tell me how to run the business I've had for decades? This place may be a shithole, but how we eat and drink is our own business. I'm too old to change. If I've done without a fridge for forty-five years, why do I need one now? Even if it makes my meat cleaner, I am not sure people's stomachs will be able to take such cleanliness!

List of Traders in Silver Village:
supplied to HFO 8 by Chief Chang

Five Metals Stall: Kwok Zidong
Noodle Stall: Wang Ming
Meat Stall: Ling Zhu
Bicycle Stall: Migrant, name unknown
Ex liquor stall, now Western-style bar:
Niu Ping
Rice and Flour Stall: Jiang Linjun
Vegetable Stall: Ma Liang
Cobbler: Rao Yun
Key Maker: Li Yin
Stationery Shop: Bao Tian
Hair Salon: Jiang Song; assistant
- migrant, name unknown
Post Office: Zhang Guofeng and
his wife
Internet Café: Song Yin and his cousin
Telephone Call Centre: Song Qing
Clothes Shop 1: Migrant, name unknown
Clothes Shop 2: Migrant, name unknown
Bookshop: Guo Feng
Electrical Goods Shop: Migrant, name
unknown
Dental Clinic: Migrant, name unknown
Motorbike Taxi Driver: Bao Mingxiang
Coca Cola Store: Li Jianhua
Petrol Pump: Zhong Ming and his wife

ID Card No: 338145365445889
Interviewer: Hunan Finance Officer 8
Date: 30 September 2013

HFO 8: So, Secretary Zhao, I can see there have been some developments since I visited your village two weeks ago.

Yes, very exciting ones, as a matter of fact. We have started building our swimming pool. In order to assist the locals, Chief Chang has brought in ten peasants from the neighbouring village. Allow me to read you the speech Chief Chang made before the official digging began:

'Silver Hill has huge potential to develop its sports facilities. We have a great deal of land and 500 children under eighteen who can build a new future for Silver Hill. It is well known that Chairman Mao swam across the Yangtze River many times in the fifties. We should train our offspring in this great tradition of swimming, and increase our reputation. Thus, I want to name this future pool: Xin Mao – New Mao Swimming Pool!'

The spot chosen for the pool is Old Kwok's land, where he used to grow chives. Maybe you have met Old Kwok, the grandfather of our UFO heroine Kwok Yun? Anyway, it seems

Old Kwok has mixed feelings about having a swimming pool dug on his land, although it has been lying fallow for many years and he now runs a 'five metals' stall. What is more, Chief Chang offered him 1000 yuan in compensation, drawn from the further budget the Provincial Government has granted to Silver Hill.

HFO 8: Old Kwok shouldn't complain. A thousand yuan is no small amount for a peasant, is it?

I don't think the money is the issue. Old Kwok wanted to keep the land. Although the soil turned bad long ago, he had been hoping one day to build a new house on it when Yun gets married and bears him a great-grandson. But I hope he convinces himself to accept the compensation. I'm sure you're right that 1000 yuan is a really good price for his land: it is more than a hundred dollars, since nowadays the dollar is going down.

The New Mao pool has also raised some other questions. When the peasants began digging, somebody asked, 'Do you know anyone here who can swim?' Everyone pondered this question, but they couldn't think of a single person who knew how to swim. 'Silver Hill is a desert,' someone said. 'How would we learn how to swim?'

When Chief Chang heard about the swimming discussions that were going on among the villagers, she modified her objectives. She has decided that she is not going to build a normal public swimming pool for our 500 children, she wants to build an Olympic-size pool for sports teams from the city. An Olympic-size pool needs to be fifty metres long and at least 2.4 metres deep, so the peasants will have to dig wider and deeper. She also plans to have a hot spa beside the pool. I don't know what that is, but if Chief Chang thinks it's important, I'm sure it is. I agree with her decision entirely. If no one in the village can swim, then the pool should be built for professional swimmers from outside. Then at least the village can earn an income from renting out the facility. Chief Chang's vision is impressive. 'The New Mao Swimming Pool will make an unforgettable mark on our soil,' she said, 'and open up our dry old ways to the dynamics of floating in a modern life.'

ID Card No: 3389787833340009
Interviewer: Hunan Finance Officer 8
Date: 30 September 2013

HFO 8: Headmaster, how are you? You look busy, but I still need to take some of your time.

Well, my next class starts in a few minutes. How can I help you?

HFO 8: After Model Peasant Kwok Yun's sighting of the UFO, your school received 2000 dollars from the United States. Furthermore, you have received another 10,000 yuan from our Education Development department. Has the government support you have received been sufficient?

No. I must say it is not sufficient at all. What we really need is ten times that amount so that we can introduce a new curriculum. Our education system is still in the Soviet style. There is too much focus on literacy because in the past we had millions of illiterate peasants, and because that was the legacy of Marxist-Leninist ideology. But I want my students to be able to contribute new ideas to our society.

This demands more than just knowing how to write: they need an education in science and technology, computing and English, so our young generation can truly catch up with the West.

HFO 8: Are you saying that we should abandon our glorious 5000-year-old tradition of writing and reading?

No, I didn't mean that. All I meant is that our education will be more effective if we reform it according to the American style, and that this will require financial support from the government. I firmly believe that, if we do this, our kids will learn to think and live globally.

HFO 8: What do you mean by 'globally'?

I mean that China will not be eaten up by American power. As our Sun Tzu said 2600 years ago in his book *The Art of War*: '*zhi ji zhi bi* – One has to understand the enemy's life first, then one can conquer the enemy.'

HFO 8: Maybe you are right, you are the headmaster after all. I think we can end here for today.

Summary of Situation in Silver Hill Village as of September 2013

REPORTING OFFICER:
Hunan Finance Officer 8

SUPERIOR OFFICER:
████████████████████████
████████████████████████

POSITIVE DEVELOPMENTS:

*   Creation and initial implementation of a Five Year Plan
*   Strong leadership and vision
*   Early signs of growth in economy and attraction of new businesses

ONGOING ISSUES:

*   Silver Hill is far behind other places in China in terms of modernisation. The level of poverty is as high as it was twenty years ago. The villagers' average yearly income is only 4000 yuan, while in China's urban areas the average income has now reached 12,000 yuan (1000 US dollars)

- Some negative response from old people who are still brooding over their bad experiences in the past

RECOMMENDATIONS:

- Continued support of this area financially, to allow Silver Hill a successful transition 'up-to-speed' status
- Encouragement of tourism
- Continued monitoring of Chief Chang's skills as a leader

FILE
Three

National Security
and Intelligence Agency
Hunan Bureau
- - - - - - - - - -

Investigation into the death of:

NAME:
Carp Li

DATE OF DEATH:
Between Sunday 3 May and Monday 4 May 2014

TIME OF DEATH:
Established by coroner as between 23:00 and 01:00

CAUSE OF DEATH:
DROWNING

AGENTS IN CHARGE:
Hunan Agent 1989; Hunan Agent 1978

1 0 MAY 2014

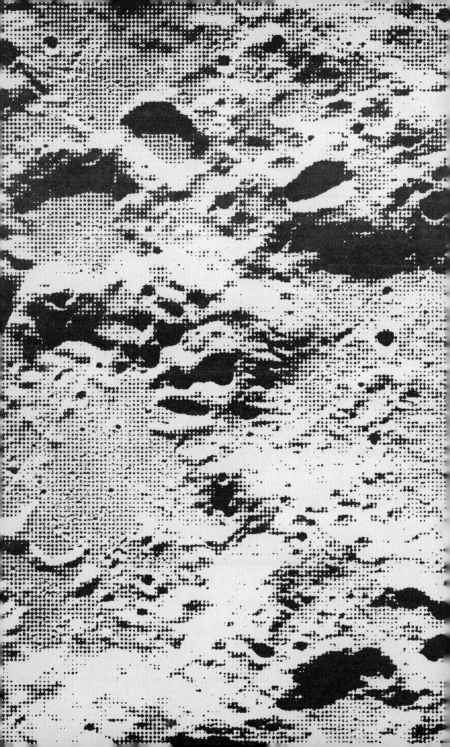

TRANSCRIPT OF INTERVIEW 001
SUBJECT: Zhao Ning
          Secretary to Chief Chang
INTERVIEW DATE: 4 May 2014
AGE: 47
SEX: Male
EDUCATION: Wen Hua Township High School
POLITICAL STATUS: Communist
FAMILY STATUS: Married; no children
ADDRESS: Pine Soil East, Silver Hill, House 036
AGENTS PRESENT: Hunan Agent 1989; Hunan Agent 1978

HN 1989: This man is always helpful, I can assure you. A very reliable witness.

HN 1978: I am glad to hear it. Secretary Zhao, Agent 1989 and I have come here to investigate Carp Li's death. Please tell us what you know.

I'm afraid I don't know much. It was a great shock for me.

His body was discovered early this morning by a group of children who passed his pond on their way to school. They saw something strange in the water, so they jumped into a canoe, and when they got closer, they recognised Carp Li's body. They immediately ran to find Headmaster Yee. To their surprise, he wasn't in the school room preparing lessons, as he always is at that time. Instead, he was pacing around the yard alone. But when he heard what they had seen, he immediately rang our office, and I myself answered the call. Half an hour later, Chief Chang and myself arrived at the pond. Other villagers were already there. Chief Chang ordered people to pull the body out of the water. It was a horrible sight. Carp Li's face was white, and his stomach swollen. We were baffled. How could a man with so much experience of water fall into his own pond, we wondered. Was he drunk?

Then Chief Chang discovered heavy stones in Carp Li's pockets. Her face lost its colour.

People started to whisper.

Chief Chang kept quiet, but I felt she was disturbed.

'Was it an accident?' Old Kwok asked in a low voice.

There was a long silence. Everybody looked at Chief Chang hoping for an answer, but she was staring at the ground.

'I suppose it is possible,' Headmaster Yee said, hesitantly, 'that he committed suicide …'

The moment the word 'suicide' was pronounced, the atmosphere turned awkward. No one knew what to think. Commit suicide! What a mad idea! To us, the idea of suicide is beyond imagination. We have lived through the most difficult times, eating grass roots or even cooking our own brothers' legs to escape starvation. And before the Great Famine, back in the forties when civil war raged through the country, life was as hard as a bullet. No one tried to commit suicide then. Why would they now, when things are getting better? How was it possible for someone to take his own life when he had already endured so much hardship? Did that not make everything he had suffered pointless? Why live in the first place?

HN 1978: What else happened before you called the police?

Only guessing and gossiping. Some people started to think about the funeral while others discussed how they should get in touch with Carp Li's son. Chief Chang interrupted their conversations to ask some questions. She is always a thorough person and she wanted to investigate Carp Li's death further. As far as she knew, she said, he was a strong, healthy man. Did he have any enemies? Everyone shook their heads. No, Carp Li had neither friends nor enemies. After his wife passed away and his son left for the city, he spent most of his time at his fish pond, as solitary as a monk. The only person he spoke to was Old Kwok.

```
TRANSCRIPT OF INTERVIEW 002
SUBJECT: Kwok Zidong (Old Kwok)
         Stall Holder
INTERVIEW DATE: 4 May 2014
AGE: 82
SEX: Male
EDUCATION: Illiterate
POLITICAL STATUS: Peasant
FAMILY STATUS: Widower (wife died 1961);
lives with granddaughter
ADDRESS: Cat Knot Pathway, Silver Hill, House 099
AGENTS PRESENT: Hunan Agent 1989; Hunan Agent 1978
```

HN 1989: Hello, Old Kwok.

You again? Every time you come, things get bad.

HN 1989: No, Granddad, you've got it wrong. It's because things
are bad that the police come. We're here to help you. Now, I need
to ask you some questions about Carp Li. It seems you were his
only friend.

Do you really have to talk to me now? What do you expect
me to say?
  Is there anything to say?

HN 1989: Well, maybe you can tell me how you felt when you heard
the news this morning.

What the hell … How did I feel? Bitch Bastard. I just stood by this pond, staring at his body until they took it away. Accident or suicide – what difference does it make? In the end, my buddy is dead, Bitch Bastard, limbs stiff, eyes shut, no more chatting, no more comforting, no more fish. This is the end, the end of the end. I don't have anything to say about it. What's the use? Qi will be transferred from one body to another. Qi never dies or disappears, so now I feel as if I am Carp Li, breathing with all his anger. And you should probably stand clear from me, young man, or you might get bad Qi from me too.

You have eyes, so I guess you can see the state of the land around this pond: cement, steel, chopped-down bushes … The Bitch Bastard place is doomed. Look at those lotuses. The flowers have just opened, but soon their pink petals will fade, their seeds will turn black, and their stems and roots will rot. This pond will be dead, dead like my sour chive patch. You policemen must have seen so many dead people. Tell me: does anybody achieve peace and contentment before they die?

TRANSCRIPT OF INTERVIEW 003
SUBJECT: **Fu Qiang (Rich and Strong)**
 Tea Farmer
INTERVIEW DATE: 4 May 2014
AGE: 64
SEX: Male
EDUCATION: Illiterate
POLITICAL STATUS: Peasant
FAMILY STATUS: Married; one son
ADDRESS: Sparrow Ditch, Silver Hill, House 078
AGENTS PRESENT: Hunan Agent 1989;
Hunan Agent 1978

HN 1989: Rich and Strong, you claim you saw Carp Li last night by his pond. Can you give me the details of what you saw?

I saw him late at night, maybe around ten or eleven. The moon was bright and reflecting in the pond, and the hills were shining silver. I was on my way home from my cousin's, a bit drunk, but I still could smell the scent of lotus coming from the pond as I stood in the bushes peeing. Then I saw Carp Li doing something very strange; he was picking up stones. He's always been a weird guy, I didn't feel like chatting to him, and I just walked home. If I'd known that he was going to … Bitch Bastard, I would have stopped and talked to him!

HN 1978: Do you know whether he had any enemies in the village?

Hmm, I don't think so.

HN 1978: Are you sure? Perhaps he had an argument with someone? Did you see him talking to anyone yesterday?

Now you remind me of something. I saw him standing at the bicycle mender's stall yesterday morning when I was walking through the market. I thought it was odd: Carp Li doesn't have a bicycle, and they can't have been having a chat because the bicycle man doesn't speak our language. Maybe you should have a word with that bicycle man, if you can get him to understand you. You can't miss him. He has a stall at the end of the market. He's always there, looking into the sky.

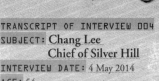

TRANSCRIPT OF INTERVIEW 004
SUBJECT: Chang Lee
        Chief of Silver Hill
INTERVIEW DATE: 4 May 2014
AGE: 54
SEX: Female
EDUCATION: Hunan Army College, Agricultural
Science Department
POLITICAL STATUS: Communist
FAMILY STATUS: Married, ████████████████████
██████████

ADDRESS: Pine Soil East, Silver Hill, House 059
AGENTS PRESENT: Hunan Agent 1989; Hunan Agent 1978

HN 1978: Chief Chang, if I'm not mistaken, your village has little experience of unusual deaths, am I right?

Unusual deaths?

HN 1978: Yes, deaths such as Carp Li's ...

I am sorry, Comrade, when you said 'unusual' I thought only of my sons. My two dead sons. Their death was unusual.

HN 1978: Is their death relevant to the death of Carp Li?

Not really. But it is relevant for me.

HN 1978: Sorry Chief Chang, but we're not here to talk about your sons. Our time is limited.

HN 1989: Perhaps we should allow her to tell us about it ...

Allow me? Yes, allow me ... Then perhaps you might go and ask questions about some of the 'unusual' deaths in this country that are never properly investigated.

In my life, I have tried not to complain about anything. I have received many benefits from the army and from the Communist Party. But I hope the Communist Party will excuse me this once for asking a question. Please tell me, how many people get killed in our mines each year?

There, you see? You don't actually know. And I bet your superiors don't know either. The problem is not whether someone in authority has the guts to tell me, the problem is that no one really cares if workers die or not. Have you ever had to investigate any case linked to a mining accident, Comrades? No? You see, I'm right. It would take up too much time, and the job of calculating the death toll is certainly not a pleasant one. Who wants it? Far better to earn quick money that you can send back to your family.

For months, Comrade, I have been searching for the official figure for the annual number of deaths in mines. I have check the *People's Daily*, I have searched through *Law Daily*, *Beijing Evening News*, *Shanghai Morning Post*, as well as *South China Weekend*, but I can't see it. Our papers only report good news, don't you think? Stories such as 'Yesterday, a fisherman caught a five-metre-long eel', or 'Last week, a

Mongolian mother gave birth to healthy triplets – two girls and one boy'. The only bad news comes from abroad. As far as I can make out from what I read, disaster belongs to the West. And when there *is* a report on a disaster in China, there are never any specific figures, no investigation, no explanation. How seriously do we actually treat death? Is it that, in fact, we have too many people in this country?

Anyway, I've been compiling my own statistics from passing references in newspapers and from the State Work Safety Adminstration's vague figures. And guess what: I've managed to work out for myself the number of miners' deaths in China last year. Do you want to know how many it was?

Well, I'll tell you anyway. More than five thousand!

Five thousand miners died in one year, in accidents ranging from gas explosions to coal-dust blasts. If that figure is close to the truth, then it makes the death of my two sons – my great contribution to the death toll – seem very insignificant.

What kind of mother was I to send two sons to the mine? How shameful for a village chief to do such a thing! I know that, with a population of nearly two billion, the death of five thousand people is not a big deal, it only means twelve deaths every day. But if you take into account the effect on the victims' mothers and wives and children, perhaps it is not such a small number in the end?

When I went to ████, the mining town where my sons died, I kept trying to imagine the last minutes of their lives. The ████████████████████████████████████

told me it was a gas explosion. It took place at 2.35 on a Wednesday afternoon. But how? It turns out the mine was run without a licence. Even though there was a small investigation after the accident, all that happened was that ███████████████████████ got sacked and was replaced by ████████████████████, who was able to pay off the local mafia. They couldn't even show me my sons' bones! They said the corpses were all fused together: fingers here, ears and toes there ... So I did this: I filled my tea bottle with black coal from that mine, took the train to Changsha holding it carefully in my hands, and then I got the bus back to Silver Hill. I poured half of the coal into an empty grave and kept half of it in the bottle. I put the bottle on a shelf. Sometimes, when I lie in my bed, I see that black coal glistening, and my ears echo with the sound of underground explosions.

My boys names? One was called Li Xing, he was nineteen, and the other was Li Dong, twenty-two. Their names are carved on their grave stones. No one has seen me crying. No one dares to talk to me about them, even my husband. It's as if they never existed. Perhaps one day I will be able to talk about them in the village, one day when I am not the Chief any more. Then I will speak about those five thousand, and the two that were my sons.

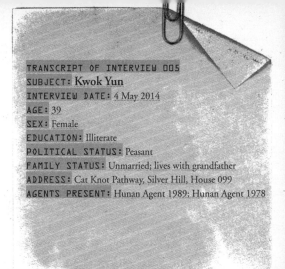

TRANSCRIPT OF INTERVIEW 005
SUBJECT: Kwok Yun
INTERVIEW DATE: 4 May 2014
AGE: 39
SEX: Female
EDUCATION: Illiterate
POLITICAL STATUS: Peasant
FAMILY STATUS: Unmarried; lives with grandfather
ADDRESS: Cat Knot Pathway, Silver Hill, House 099
AGENTS PRESENT: Hunan Agent 1989; Hunan Agent 1978

HN 1989: Kwok Yun, I hope you can help us to find a man.

Who?

HN 1989: A witness saw Carp Li standing at the bike mender's stall yesterday morning, but we've searched the whole market and the bike mender doesn't seem to be there.

Oh …

HN 1989: People say that you are often at his stall. Do you know where he might have gone?

No, no I don't … But why are you looking for him? You don't think he had something to do with Carp Li's death do you?

I'm sure he didn't. The bicycle mender is a good person. He is quiet, or you city people might say he has good manners. In Silver Hill, nobody has good manners.

HN 1989: Do you know his name?

No. We don't know anything about him. He's a migrant.

HN 1978: Kwok Yun, you seem troubled. Are you holding anything back? May I remind you of your duty to hide nothing from the People's Police.

HN 1989: Don't be scared, Kwok Yun. Tell us what you know.

Well, it's just that a few days ago, I had a conversation with the bicycle mender. It was very strange.

I went to his stall to get a spoke fixed. He took a long time to do the repair and while he was working I sat on the ground staring at the hills. I thought about how the harsh sun cut the hills in two, putting one half in dark shadow, the other half in bright light. Then I thought about how, before my lessons with Headmaster Yee, I had very little idea what lay beyond those hills. Suddenly the words sprang out of my mouth:

'Where are you from?'

I was really surprised by myself. Why would I ask such a thing? And what did it matter to me where he came from? Anyway he didn't react. But still, I insisted:

'I've heard you are from the North.'

The bicycle mender was putting the wheel back in place. He didn't seem to have heard my question.

You know, before I saw the UFO, I never asked questions. But now it seems as if my life is one big question. Anyway, I asked another one.

'In the North where?'

And then – even Heaven hadn't expected that – he answered:

'A place called Desert Wind.'

I was dumbstruck. His voice was deep and husky, and his accent very unusual. I'd never heard someone speak like that before.

'Desert Wind?' I repeated the name like a fool. 'Where is that?'

And can you believe it? The silent man spoke again!

'It is a town in Ji Lin Province where everything lies under a blanket of snow.'

A blanket of snow. I tried to imagine what that would look like. Suddenly I had a great desire to see snow – to walk and walk until I found some.

'Do you miss your home town?' I asked. But the bicycle mender didn't answer. He just kept his head down while he finished his work. Then he washed his hands in his basin of oily water and gave me back my bicycle.

HN 1989: Did he say anything else?

Nothing. He was as quiet as a leaf. I handed him three yuan. He just lit a cigarette with his pale fingers, and sat on his bench to rest. As I rode away, he was motionless, as if he was wrapped in a daydream, just gazing at the tools in his old wooden toolbox.

HN 1989: And when did you last see him?

That was the last time. I wanted to go and see him today. The spoke he put in has already come loose ...

HN 1978: And what were you doing yesterday? Did you see Carp Li?

No, I didn't see Carp Li. Yesterday was ... just like any other day.

TRANSCRIPT OF INTERVIEW 006
SUBJECT: Ling Zhu
        Ex-butcher
INTERVIEW DATE: 4 May 2014
AGE: 67
SEX: Male
EDUCATION: Illiterate
POLITICAL STATUS: Peasant
FAMILY STATUS: Married; one son; lives alone
ADDRESS: Sparrow Ditch, Silver Hill, House 033
AGENTS PRESENT: Hunan Agent 1989; Hunan Agent 1978

HN 1989: Old Ling, can I interrupt your game of chess to ask you some questions?

What do you want this time? Can't you leave me in peace? Don't you think you've had enough from me? After twenty years of wielding my knife, all I can wield now are these plastic chess pieces. Don't say you want to take these away too.

HN 1978: You must answer our questions!

Ask your colleague there why I don't like the police. When he last visited this village, I had a famous butcher's stall. Now I sit all day outside the Old People's Palace with nothing to do. Cow's Cunt! They took my stall away from me because they thought that I, a famous Parasite Eradication Hero, couldn't get rid of a few flies!

HN 1978: That is nothing to do with us. We are here to investigate the death of Carp Li.

I've got nothing to say about it.

HN 1978: I will say again – you are obliged to answer our questions. Now listen. Since you sit here all day, watching the world go by, you must observe what is going on in the market. Did you see Carp Li talk to the bicycle mender yesterday morning?

No.

HN 1978: And have you seen the bicycle mender recently?

No. But I'm glad he's gone. We don't want strangers in this village.

HN 1978: Did you ever see Model Peasant Kwok Yun visit the bicycle mender?

Her? She's the start of it all. If it wasn't for her, I'd still have my stall, and our market wouldn't be overrun by foreigners.

HN 1978: I repeat – we are not here to discuss the issue of your stall, so please answer the question. Did you ever see Model Peasant Kwok Yun visit the bicycle mender?

Of course I did! She was at his fucking stall all the time. I tell you, Old Kwok's granddaughter is as attracted to that bicycle mender as a fly to a piece of pork. And I'd say he's interested in her too. I once saw him fix her bell. I was nearby, smoking my pipe, and I heard her tell him that her bell was so rusty it hadn't rung for years. What happened then was amazing. The man just touched her bell with those pale, weak hands of his, and immediately it rang.

'Cow's Cunt, if that's not love ...' I murmured to myself. And on top of that, she smiled at him! Let me tell you: I've never seen that woman smile before.

HN 1978: How did the bicycle man react to her smile?

I wasn't looking at him. I was looking at Kwok Yun and thinking she wasn't a bad piece of flesh when she smiled. Somehow she didn't seem so masculine. Then she realised I was staring at her and cycled off.

HN 1978: From what you observed, do you think they might have been having a relationship?

Cow's Cunt! A relationship? I wouldn't want to talk about Kwok Yun and her relationships. It might ruin the family reputation. You are the police, you know best, I listen to you. Now, tell me: how can I get my stall back?

Needs further questioning

TRANSCRIPT OF INTERVIEW 007
SUBJECT: Yee Ming
        Headmaster of Primary School
INTERVIEW DATE: 4 May 2014
AGE: 51
SEX: Male
EDUCATION: Changsha Normal College, Maths Department
POLITICAL STATUS: Communist
FAMILY STATUS: Unmarried
ADDRESS: Primary School, Silver Hill
AGENTS PRESENT: Hunan Agent 1989; Hunan Agent 1978

HN 1978: Headmaster Yee, we have been told that you behaved in an uncharacteristic manner this morning. Instead of preparing your lessons, you were pacing around the school yard. Why was that?

It's true that I usually get up early to prepare lessons before the children arrive, but last night I couldn't sleep and, when dawn came, I needed to walk.

HN 1978: Was there any particular reason why you couldn't sleep?

Sorry, could you repeat the question.

HN 1978: Was there any particular reason why you couldn't sleep?

Oh … no.

161

HN 1978: You didn't see Carp Li at all yesterday?

No.

HN 1978: Who did you see?

No one. I stayed in the school all day … Although Kwok Yun came in the afternoon for a lesson.

HN 1978: You mean the woman who saw the UFO? Isn't she too old for lessons?

Yes. No. Well … it was Chief Chang's idea … After the UFO incident, she tried to … to educate Yun.

HN 1978: Educate?

Yes, teach her to read and write. 'Yun has become very important for Silver Hill,' she told me, 'but she's still illiterate, and that's certainly not good either for her future or for our links with the outside world. So I'd like you to help her learn. Why don't you give her some private tuition when you have some free time?'

I hesitated a bit, since my normal teaching keeps me very busy already, but in the end I agreed. Chief Chang brought her to the school the following Sunday.

'You both have a lot in common,' she told us. 'As Confucius said: "Independence at thirty; clarity at forty; certainty at fifty." I think you two should waste no more time.'

Then she went back to her office, leaving Kwok Yun with me. I felt very awkward. Neither of us knew what to say ... I made some tea, and we drank it ...

HN 1978: And?

Well ... I told her she could come to the school every Sunday afternoon.

HN 1978: And so she came yesterday ...

Yes, she did.

HN 1978: And what did you teach her?

I ... I taught her to write the character for 'snow' 雪 (*xue*). It may not seem very useful for a woman who lives in such a hot place to be able to write about snow, but she asked me to teach her. 'Have you ever seen the snow, Headmaster Yee?' she asked. She thinks that, because I studied in Changsha, I have seen the world. 'How does snow feel?' she wanted to know. 'Like goose feathers falling? Does it look like white sugar powder?' I told her everything I knew about snow. She is a fast learner, compared to other adults.

HN 1978: And did she ask any other unusual questions?

Actually, she did. She asked me if I'd ever been to Ji Lin Province. I couldn't think why she would ask such a thing, so

I said to her, 'Kwok Yun, you should concentrate on learning things that will be useful to you in your role as Model Peasant, so that you can build a future in this village.' And we carried on with the lesson.

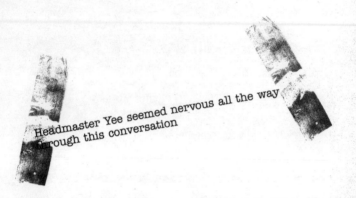

Headmaster Yee seemed nervous all the way through this conversation

TRANSCRIPT OF INTERVIEW 008
SUBJECT: Kwok Yun
INTERVIEW DATE: 5 May 2014
AGE: 39
SEX: Female
EDUCATION: Illiterate
POLITICAL STATUS: Peasant
FAMILY STATUS: Unmarried; lives with grandfather
ADDRESS: Cat Knot Pathway, Silver Hill, House 099
AGENTS PRESENT: Hunan Agent 1989; Hunan Agent 1978

HN 1978: Kwok Yun, it has come to our attention that you have been dishonest in answering our questions. When asked about your movements yesterday, you said it was 'just like any other day', and yet we have learned from Headmaster Yee that you were having a lesson at the school. Do you do that every day?

Yes … I mean, no. Only on Sundays.

HN 1978: You must know it is a crime to obstruct a police investigation. It amounts to collaboration in crime. Perhaps you think that my colleague here is soft, but you can't get past me.

I don't want to obstruct you … But even if I did go to see Headmaster Yee, what does it matter to you?

HN 1978: Everything matters to us. Is there something you are trying to hide?

...

HN 1978: Speak. You're wasting our time.

I feel so ashamed.

HN 1989: Kwok Yun, a police investigation is a secret procedure, nobody will know what you have told us. And according to the law, you have to answer. Don't make us threaten you ...

Okay ...

It's right that I went to the school yesterday, as I always do on Sunday. But it wasn't the same as usual. Headmaster Yee seemed nervous.

Anyway, when I got to the school, he told me to get a calligraphy brush and copy some characters. I asked him to teach me the character for 'snow' but I couldn't concentrate. My mind kept wandering and I made ink blots on the page. Then, at a certain moment, Headmaster Yee turned to me and said, 'Kwok Yun, I think you should concentrate on learning things that will be useful to you in your role as Model Peasant, so that you can build a future in this village.'

'What sort of useful things?' I asked.

But he didn't answer, and then ...

HN 1989: You must report everything to us honestly, and in detail.

Well, I thought my first man would at least kiss me. But he didn't. Then I reminded myself: 'I'm nearly forty and I'm ugly. Why would a man want to kiss me?' All he said was, 'Shall we try?' And I said, 'OK.'

HN 1989: Is that really all he said?

Yes.

I had no idea what I should do. I lay down on the bed and he sat beside me. My bowels were in pain, like a balloon above fire. I could feel the noodles I had eaten for lunch struggling and swimming in my miserable stomach, and I was worried the headmaster could hear the horrible noises as those noodles tried to dig their way further and deeper into my dark tubes and tunnels. I felt like hiding under the bed. But I stayed there.

'Just let him do whatever he is going to do to me!' I told myself. 'We have to go through this! If we don't, it will be too late. Too late for everything. Too late to have a family, to have children. Too late to start my life. And most important of all, too late for my grandfather. He could die any day. For him, I have to hurry up.'

So I lay flat on Headmaster Yee's bed, tense, like a duck facing the knife. I wanted to get things done quickly. No messing around, no wasting life.

HN 1989: And then?

The headmaster was so timid. More than I was, maybe. He tried to open the buttons on my shirt, but his fingers were stiff, he couldn't do it. I thought that he maybe had never unbuttoned a woman's shirt before. He wasn't married. Perhaps he was just like me and had never got to know the business between a man and a woman.

It was taking too long, I was soaked in shame. Eventually I had to get up from his bed and take off my own trousers and underpants. And he was still fully dressed. We both felt very awkward and nervous. I was worrying that some kid might walk in with a maths question. He must have read my anxiety because he got up and went to check that the door was locked. He seemed lost. He came back to my body. And then he removed his grey shirt with its dirty collar, and unzipped his blue worker's trousers which he wears in all seasons.

A naked man … I was astonished. He had very pale skin, much fairer than most peasants. There was no sunburn, no insect bites, no scars on his body. His milky skin was smoother than mine. Again, I felt ashamed of myself. My body didn't match his, and I couldn't match his knowledge and his kindness either.

While he was on top of me, I tried to think about something else. There was a maths problem written in white chalk on the blackboard above the bed. The final line stuck in my mind

Minus one. I repeated that number to myself, again and again, as Yee was moving above me. 'What is minus one? Am I like a minus, a number of insufficiency, a symbol of debt from my last incarnation?' Officer, you tell me!

We didn't say anything to each other. A strong force penetrated me and held me tight; I felt pain in my lower body. I couldn't breathe. But I was happy. Now my grandfather can stop worrying, I thought. Finally, I have done something for him.

Conclusions from investigation into death of Carp Li

REPORTING OFFICER:
Hunan Agent 1978

DATE:
6 May 2014

Having conducted a number of interviews in Silver Hill, Hunan Agent 1989 and myself are agreed that the cause of Carp Li's death was suicide. No one in the village had a motive to do him harm, particularly not a financial one since his fish farm was due to be closed down, and he was a poor man. The stones in his pocket seem to rule out accidental death. Furthermore, a number of factors may have influenced his decision to take his own life:

1. *Loneliness: his wife is dead and his son lives in Changsha.*
2. *Depression: the villagers' descriptions of him as taciturn suggest he was mentally ill.*
3. *Fear of future change: we understand he was unhappy about recent developments in the village and had refused to embrace Chief Chang's Five Year Plan. This suggests low intelligence. He clearly lacked the ability to adjust to the demands of the modern world.*

The only outstanding question regards what Carp Li said to the bicycle mender in the market on the morning of Sunday 3 May. We have not been able to locate the bicycle mender. Our research into Ji Lin Province has not revealed a place called 'Desert Wind', which, according to Model Peasant Kwok Yun, was the name of the bicycle mender's home town. Either it doesn't exist, or it is a very small place bearing a different official name. There is also the possibility that it is beyond the North Korean border, since people in Ji Lin Province are known to live in Korean areas. Though we questioned peasants on the roads out of Silver Hill, none had seen the bicycle mender pass. Since we do not believe it will influence our findings, we suggest this line of inquiry be dropped.

National Security
and Intelligence Agency
Hunan Bureau
- - - - - - - - - - - -

The 09-11-2012 UFO Case Update

FILE
Four

CASE START DATE:
11 September 2012

CASE END DATE:
Still in progress

UPDATE:
September 2015

OPERATIVES IN CHARGE:
Beijing Agent 1919 & Hunan Agent 1989

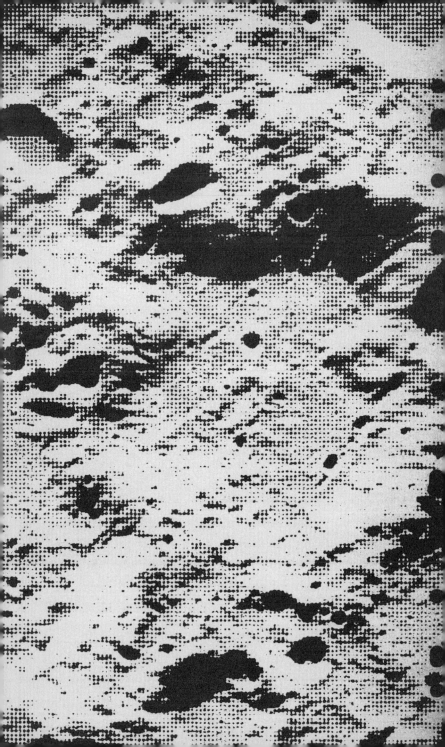

TRANSCRIPT OF INTERVIEW 001
SUBJECT: Zhao Ning
         Director of the Silver Hill
         History Museum
INTERVIEW DATE: 11 September 2015
AGE: 48
SEX: Male
EDUCATION: Wen Hua Township High School
POLITICAL STATUS: Communist
FAMILY STATUS: Divorced
ADDRESS: 25 New Star Drive, Silver Hill
AGENTS PRESENT: Beijing Agent 1919; Hunan Agent 1989

BJ 1919: Mr Zhao, as you know the Security Agency has kept a close eye on Silver Hill since the appearance of the UFO in 2012. I want an update on what's been happening in your village, or should I now say town … Let's start with the UFO. Have there been any further sightings?

The UFO? Time passes so quickly. There have been many changes here since then. I, for instance, am divorced. It's strange living alone, although I am seeing a woman who is a migrant from Hu Bei Province. I hope she will bear me a child. And you, Officer? You seem to have put on a bit of weight: your life must be nicer now? Have you been promoted?

BJ 1919: Just because you got a promotion, don't think everyone else has. But tell us about Kwok Yun. I don't have much time.

Well, I haven't had any contact with Yun and her family for a long time. I've been very busy. When I am not assisting Chief Chang, I spend most of my time arranging the exhibits at our new museum. In fact, the last time I saw Yun was at her wedding. She got married two months ago, and the wedding banquet was organised by Chief Chang at our new restaurant, UFO's Favorite. Have you seen the place? It's the one with the pink neon sign on the roof, so bright that even aeroplanes can see it at night. It's owned by the Chow Mein King. Last year he closed down his stall and put together all his savings to build a restaurant next to the highway where the cars now pass and lift clouds of red dust. The house speciality is Beef Chow Mein. It's very good, I promise you, you should go there before you leave.

The banquet was held on a Sunday afternoon, when the headmaster was able to take time off work. There were fifty round tables – twenty inside the restaurant and thirty outside. It was like New Year's festival. Kids were chasing each other around, and the fireworks never stopped.

Kwok Yun didn't seem to know how to behave. She wore a red cheongsam which, on her square and bulky frame, looked, shall I say unusual. Her face was blank, as if she was suffocating in the high collar of her tight dress. The headmaster had at last abandoned his blue worker's trousers and wore a new suit. They sat together in the middle of the guests looking uncomfortable, their backs as straight as two doors. Every ten seconds they had to stand up to receive more congratulations.

Only Chief Chang remained sober. Here, let me find my transcript of her speech.

> *Please allow me to say a few words on this significant occasion. Today is an extremely important day for Silver Hill. We are here to celebrate two things. First, this perfect union between Headmaster Yee and Kwok Yun. They cherish the same ideals and have a common goal: to play an effective role in the village's modernisation. We hope they will be together for ever and soon have a beautiful and clever child!*

Everyone applauded, and more firecrackers were lit. Then Chief Chang continued:

> *Secondly, I have some good news to announce: given the outstanding qualities that Yun showed three years ago – seeing a UFO and saving the life of an important American dignitary – the Provincial Tourism Office has decided to invite both her and her husband to work in the capital city Changsha!*

This news took everybody by surprise. Not me, of course. I had seen how hard Chief Chang had been working to organise such prestigious jobs for Yun and Headmaster Yee. For several weeks she had been calling everyone she knew in

Changsha to try to pull strings. I watched as the guests came over to congratulate the newlyweds. Yun was very silent and let her husband do all the talking. As for Old Kwok, he carried on drinking with whoever raised their glass to him. But he didn't seem happy to me. Later, I went to speak to him. 'I've spent half of my life dreaming about building a big house on my chive patch,' he said, 'and having my granddaughter and her child living in it. And look at me now: first, I lose my land to a swimming pool, and now, not only does my granddaughter marry that teacher, but suddenly she has to go and work in the city. Which Bitch Bastard city office needs her, I ask you?'

I told him he should be grateful for Chief Chang's huge generosity. She saw her two sons die from manual labour yet she was helping his daughter get a good office job so that she could be comfortable for the rest of her life and not have to toil under the boiling sun.

He just looked at me and drank another bottle of beer.

Perhaps when our villagers visit my museum, they will understand everything that Chief Chang has done for them. If you look at the section devoted to Chief Chang's Five Year Plan, you will see that, despite recent disturbances, we are certain to achieve our goals by 2018.

TRANSCRIPT OF INTERVIEW 002
SUBJECT: Wong Jing
        Rice Farmer
INTERVIEW DATE: 11 September 2015
AGE: 43
SEX: Male
EDUCATION: Illiterate
POLITICAL STATUS: Peasant
FAMILY STATUS: Married; two children
ADDRESS: 101 New Power Garden Villas, Silver Hill
AGENTS PRESENT: Beijing Agent 1919; Hunan Agent 1989

HN 1989: Hello again, Old Wong. Tell us. Have there been any further signs of UFO activity in your rice fields?

Rice fields? What Bitch Bastard rice fields? Have you got two eyes? I tell you they don't exist any more. My rice fields lie underneath those factories over there – and that tourism centre with its stupid museum and its big empty carpark. What do they need such a big carpark for anyway? No one ever goes there. But it's ruined my life. I'm not the only one either. Take a look at Rich and Strong these days. Bitch Bastard! They make us live in these blocks of flats where you have to climb ten flights of stairs just to get to your front door. Mad old Liu Shi didn't even make it. 'How will my husband find me here?' she cried when they took her to her new home, and dropped down dead. And you ask me about

UFO activity? Bitch Bastard! That Kwok Yun walks around like a city person now, with her city clothes, her education and her new husband, but she has built her fortune on my misfortune. Women! You know they will ruin your life right from the start. Bitch Bastard women!

TRANSCRIPT OF INTERVIEW 003
SUBJECT: **Kwok Zidong (Old Kwok)**
        Stall Holder
INTERVIEW DATE: 11 September 2015
AGE: 83
SEX: Male
EDUCATION: Illiterate
POLITICAL STATUS: Peasant
FAMILY STATUS: Widower (wife died 1961); lives alone
ADDRESS: Cat Knot Pathway, Silver Hill, House 099
AGENTS PRESENT: Beijing Agent 1919; Hunan Agent 1989

HN 1989: Congratulations on your granddaughter's marriage, Old Kwok. I hope you don't feel too lonely now that she's living with her husband.

Lonely? What kind of weird question is that? Yes I feel lonely, if that's the answer you want from an old man. I didn't feel like this before, not even when my wife died. But now I do.

Still, you can't change your fate – it's arranged by Heaven. Everyone is born alone, everyone dies alone. If there's one thing I've learned in my Bitch Bastard eighty-three years, it's that. Yun says, 'Granddad, we'll come back to see you every three or four months.' But I know there are certain things in this world you can't count on. They'll come back all right, but it will be for my funeral. And it won't change the fact that I'll be lying alone in my cold grave.

What else can I tell you? It's Chrysanthemum Month. All I want to do is walk down to the graveyard and sit beside those yellow flowers, so that I can spend some time with my elders. In that world I will meet those vanished faces and hear the echo of their distant voices.

I often think of Carp Li. He did the right thing. A wise man. Why carry on eating rice every day? It is just a waste. A waste of food.

BJ 1919: Chief Chang, since my last visit three years ago, we have been hearing a great deal about your region. We have been very impressed by the progress here. But a few days ago there was some negative news ...

First, have some Oolong. We didn't harvest much tea this year, as there are not many farmers left to work on their land. Nevertheless, I saved some good leaves for you.

Yes ... I'm afraid I had to report some bad news. There has been a riot. Earlier this week, some citizens started to protest about our new mobile phone factory. They claim it has been built on unfairly seized land. Well ... the situation seems to be deteriorating ... I feel deeply embarrassed that our people still haven't understood the price that has to be paid to build a strong and civilised society.

BJ 1919: As village chief, you must control the situation and keep the media away from this area. You understand?

I know. That's why we've asked that your security forces come down here and ensure safety, so that the building work can continue. We've also sent two trucks with loudspeakers through the town to discourage people from protesting.

BJ 1919: We will sort this out. In the meantime you must immediately draw up a list of the potential threats to the economic development of your village, sorry your *town*. Now, is there anything else you want to tell us?

Apart from this unfortunate incident, everything is moving in a very positive direction. The construction of the highway continues day and night. We now have a sports centre, a bank, a shopping mall, a tourism centre with museum, and a hotel. Most of the old houses have been demolished.

Regrettably, we have had to cut down our three Hundred Arm trees, as they were standing in the way of the modernisation work. It's a pity, as many people were attached to those trees, but there was no way around it. As we say: lose a tree, gain a forest. Our town can afford such a sacrifice, which will appear small in the light of our much brighter future. And now I can say with certainty that, by 2018, we will have achieved all the goals in our Five Year Plan.

Let me tell you about my next project: I have been in contact with our friend Huang Lingdong, the power-generator millionaire who wrote a best-selling English text book, and I'm very hopeful he will agree to build his biggest ever factory in our town. I already have a spot in mind for it: Rich and Strong's tea fields. He's working at the supermarket now, so he doesn't need them. The supermarket is a good workplace for him. He didn't understand this at first, but he has an open mind and the desire to become a good citizen and so I'm sure he will become a very successful cleaner.

I am extremely proud that we have been able to achieve today's results! And I'm convinced that, in the very near future, Silver Hill will live up to its name and become a place where you will truly find silver on the streets. We aim to be a launch pad for the future of China. Soon, every citizen will be able to travel the world, to see the *Mona Lisa* and the Alhambra, and even possibly to start amazing voyages into Outer Space.

TRANSCRIPT OF INTERVIEW 005
SUBJECT: Yee Ming
            Headmaster of Primary School
INTERVIEW DATE: 11 September 2015
AGE: 52
SEX: Male
EDUCATION: Changsha Normal College, Maths Department
POLITICAL STATUS: Communist
FAMILY STATUS: Married; no children
ADDRESS: 50 Moon Avenue, Silver Hill
AGENTS PRESENT: Beijing Agent 1919; Hunan Agent 1989

BJ 1919: Dog Sun, you've got yourself an interesting wife. She must be the most famous person in Silver Hill! Bet you're glad you're getting out of here though. Okay, this village, sorry, *town*, isn't the poxy place it used to be, but still ...

Anyway, we're grateful that you ask your pupils to keep an eye on the sky for us. Has there been any UFO activity?

As you see, we keep these careful records, but there has been nothing. All the children have seen are more aeroplanes. And sometimes the smog from the factory chimneys is so thick they can't see anything. But I'm afraid I must get on now. My wife and I leave for Changsha in two days' time so there is a lot to prepare. The teacher who is taking my place arrives tomorrow. Unlike me, he is an IT specialist. Chief Chang felt that it was important for the children to learn how to apply the pure maths I teach in this school. In Changsha, I shall work in the accounts department of the Provincial Tourism Office where Chief Chang in her great generosity has found me a job.

BJ 1919: Okay, I'll let you go. I hope you enjoy the city with all its karaoke bars and nightlife. Knowledge will be much more useful to you there. Good luck, Headmaster.

TRANSCRIPT OF INTERVIEW 006
SUBJECT: Kwok Yun
INTERVIEW DATE: 11 September 2015
AGE: 40
SEX: Female
EDUCATION: Equivalent to high-school level
POLITICAL STATUS: Peasant
FAMILY STATUS: Married; no children
ADDRESS: 50 Moon Avenue, Silver Hill
AGENTS PRESENT: Beijing Agent 1919; Hunan Agent 1989

HN 1989: Congratulations on your marriage, Kwok Yun. You must be very happy living in this new apartment block. I hope you have also found a good place to live in Changsha? Can you give us an update on what's been happening to you?

What do you want to know now? Have you not investigated my whole life already?

BJ 1919: Dog Sun! Don't start this again. Just tell us what we need to know so we can get out of here. We have an important meeting with Chief Chang.

HN 1989: Let me talk to her. I'll meet you back at the village. I know you insist we carry out interviews together, but in an emergency like this, we can override the protocols ...

Note: Beijing Agent 1919 left after first five minutes of interview believing subject would talk more freely without him.

Now, Kwok Yun, perhaps with my colleague gone you'll find it easier to say what you want to say.

I haven't got anything to tell you. Ever since my wedding, I've felt ill. My throat is blocked and I cough all the time. The doctor says it's to do with the heavy pollution in Silver Hill.

HN 1989: Tell me about the wedding.

What a day! Unbearable! At one point, I couldn't take it any more, I had to leave the banquet and be alone. I don't know how long it was before they noticed I was gone. I didn't care, to be honest. I felt much better once I was on my own. I walked and walked. The hills in the distance appeared silver-blue. Clouds were gathering and the dusk brought with it a cool wind. I tried to take deep breaths. Luckily, I didn't faint.

I was still in shock from the news Chief Chang had announced. I was struggling with all kinds of conflicting thoughts. Even today, I can't believe it. Do I really have to live in a big city with my husband? Even if I don't really like it here in Silver Hill, still, I know every inch of this village as well as I know my own skin. I've watched it change since the UFO event, seen it grow new roads and buildings, seen migrants come and go. But now I'm going to leave, leave my grandfather, and work in an office in the city. And there, I will know nobody and no place. I will be a stranger, like our bicycle mender was. It's as if I'm a cicada who, in order to grow into an adult, has to slough off her skin and leave it behind. You understand what I mean?

HN 1989: If you think back to the experience of seeing the UFO, what comes into your mind?

It has been a long while since I last thought of the UFO. But on the evening of my wedding, when I was walking alone, I passed what used to be Wong's rice fields and found myself standing in front of the monument – you know, the one Chief Chang erected to commemorate what I witnessed. But somehow the shape of the sculpture didn't look anything like the flying thing I saw. I remember something completely different – not round and flat, not even white. I began to feel confused. Then I left the monument, and wandered through the carpark. As I walked along, I stumbled on something. I looked down. It was the root of a Hundred Arm tree. 'Oh,' I thought, 'this must be the only bit left of our Hundred Arm trees. They've dug up all the rest. And it was in these roots that I fainted three years ago, when I saw the UFO.' I looked down at the root curling through the soil, and at the columns of ants crawling around it, and I thought about how helpless we are in this village – just like those ants: desperate and powerless.

And in the end I arrived at Carp Li's old fish pond, which is now part of the provincial canal. The water was black and smelt of rot. The lotuses were gone. I was glad that Carp Li shut his eyes before seeing this dreadful scene, otherwise he wouldn't have been able to find peace in the Shady Place.

I sat down on the concrete bank, wishing I could see a fish. Then I imagined a red carp swimming in the water, playing between the weeds and the lotus roots. At that moment, a full moon rose in the east, and I saw my reflection in the water. A breeze came and broke my image, then slowly it formed again. I realised I was indeed leaving this place, and, for the first time in my life that I can remember, tears came to my eyes.

The 09-11-2012 UFO Case
Summary of Findings

DRAFTED BY:
Beijing Agent 1919

REPORT DATE:
20 September 2015

Because of the State of Emergency in Silver Hill during the period of this investigation, it must be noted that findings are partial. Peasant rioting escalated while interviews were taking place and Hunan Agent 1989 lost his life while trying to reach the safety of the village chief's office. Cause of death: bullet wound from a shotgun fired by Butcher Ling Zhu. Butcher Ling had obtained a shotgun from a certain Jiang Hui, recently returned from military service in the provincial army, and fired indiscriminately into a building site, injuring ▮ construction workers and killing ▮▮▮▮▮▮▮▮▮▮. Hunan Agent 1989 was caught in the hail of bullets and was shot in the chest. Chief Chang has now been removed as village leader. Considering her undeniable contribution to Silver Hill, she will be granted a pension of 2000 yuan per month, and she and her husband will have free access to the village's new facilities. A replacement, a young man, will be brought in from Changsha. Ling and Jiang have received prison sentences.

From interviews conducted with Kwok Yun and those who know her, it appears that she has had no further contact with extraterrestrial phenomena. She is leading a normal life. In fact, there have been noticeable improvements in her living conditions. Getting married and being given a job in the city have improved her confidence and self-image. It is therefore suggested that the '09-11-2012 UFO Case' be closed, but that Kwok Yun be made a State Witness, 人证: as such she will join the group of dissidents, criminals and notable citizens who are under permanent surveillance. It is in the interests of China that a record be kept of her history.

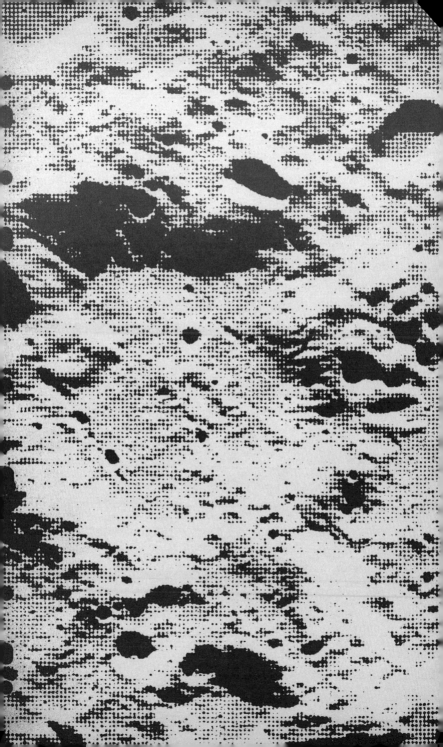

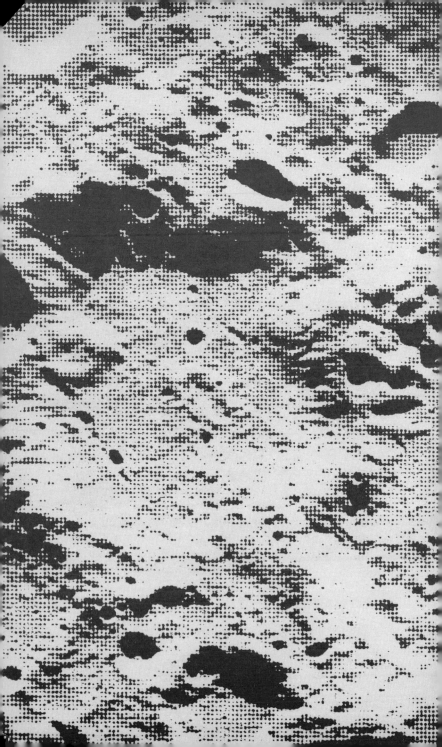

UFO sightings in China during 2012

WHERE:	Mao Zidong High School, Changping, Hebei Province
WHEN:	15 March, 16:06
BY WHOM:	Four male pupils (Zheng Li, Liang Jian, Wei Ren, Yu Jiping)
DESCRIPTION:	Pulsing green lights starting high in the sky and moving downwards over period of an hour
INVESTIGATION RESULT:	Malfunction of laser lights in nearby sports stadium

WHERE:	Bao Tou, Inner Mongolia
WHEN:	8 May, approx 11:40
BY WHOM:	Bao Linping
DESCRIPTION:	Flying white disc nearby Bao Tou Airport, appearing and disappearing several times, lasting about 15 minutes
INVESTIGATION RESULT:	Possible air and steam reflections through clouds above Gobi Desert in the north

WHERE:	Nagri County, Tibet
WHEN:	10 July, approx 19:30
BY WHOM:	Norbu and his wife Rinjing
DESCRIPTION:	Small white flashing circle that disappeared after 10 minutes
INVESTIGATION RESULT:	Military signals sent from Pakistan border

WHERE:	Silver Hill Village, Hunan Province
WHEN:	11 September, approx 12:00
BY WHOM:	Kwok Yun
DESCRIPTION:	Flying metal disc above rice fields
INVESTIGATION RESULT:	Unresolved

List of Main Witnesses (in order of age)

Liu Shi, female, born 1930
ID Card No. 3326782220009

Kwok Zidong (Old Kwok), male, born 1932
ID Card No. 338768742234441

Li Sheng (Carp Li), male, born 1941
ID Card No. 334345239004934

Ling Zhu, male, born 1947
ID Card No. 3345567355698887

Fu Qiang (Rich and Strong), male, born 1950
ID Card No. 335656787856772

Chang Lee (Chief Chang), female, born 1960
ID Card No. 331643343886009

Yee Ming (Headmaster Yee), male, born 1962
ID Card No. 3389787833340009

Zhao Ning (Secretary Zhao), male, born 1967
ID Card No. 338145365445889

Wong Jing, male, born 1971
ID Card No. 334565334229008

Kwok Yun, female, born 1975
ID Card No. 331248672238784

APPENDIX 3

Key Events in Recent Chinese History

1927–1949: Civil war between Kuomintang & Communist Party

1949: Socialist Revolution succeeds

1950–1953: The Korean War

1951: The Liberation of Tibet

1953–1957: China's First Five Year Plan

1958–1960: The Great Leap Forward

1959–1962: Three Years of Disaster and Famine

1966–1976: The Cultural Revolution

1967: Death of Last Emperor Pu Yi

1976: Death of Mao Zedong

1978: Beginning of Deng Xiaoping's Economic Reform

1979: Introduction of the One Child Policy

1997: Death of Deng Xiaoping

2001: China joins the World Trade Organisation

2008: China host the Olympic Games for the first time

2010: 700 million peasants remain in rural China

2012: UFO is sighted in Silver Hill